The Harvesters

The Harvesters

Jasmina Odor

A NOVEL

Freehand Books gratefully acknowledges the financial support for its publishing program provided by the Canada Council for the Arts and the Alberta Media Fund, and by the Government of Canada through the Canada Book Fund.

This book is available in print and Global Certified Accessible™ EPUB formats.

Freehand Books is located in Moh'kinsstis, Calgary, Alberta, within Treaty 7 territory and Métis Nation of Alberta Region 3, and on the traditional territories of the Siksika, the Kainai, and the Piikani, as well as the Iyarhe Nakoda and Tsuut'ina nations.

FREEHAND BOOKS
freehand-books.com

LIBRARY AND ARCHIVES CANADA CATALOGUING IN PUBLICATION
Title: The harvesters / Jasmina Odor.
Names: Odor, Jasmina, author.
Identifiers:
  Canadiana (print) 20240286707
  Canadiana (ebook) 20240286715
  ISBN 9781990601613 (softcover)
  ISBN 9781990601620 (EPUB)
  ISBN 9781990601637 (PDF)
Subjects: LCGFT: Novels.
Classification: LCC PS8629.D67 H37 2024 | DDC C813/.6—dc23

Edited by Deborah Willis
Design by Natalie Olsen
Cover photo © Kara Riley / Stocksy
Author photo by Trisia Eddy
Printed and bound in Canada

FIRST PRINTING

Canada
Canada Council for the Arts — Conseil des Arts du Canada
Alberta Government

This, after all, is aftermath, the second harvest:
life with knowledge of what has gone before.

RACHEL CUSK, *AFTERMATH*

MIRA AND BERNARD'S hotel is one street up from Boulevard Saint-Germain and a quick walk to the Notre Dame, which explains why it's not cheap, despite the one-star rating. They rent bikes at one of the bike stations and ride up, into streets away from the boulevard, around the Sorbonne, west, Mira following Bernard's lead happily. She takes in the repetition of curved balcony railings, the hints of courtyards, the street names she'll never remember later. The sun comes and goes. To ride a bike on these quiet streets, leisurely, feeling small undulations under the wheels, following this dear person she doesn't get to see as much as she would like, is ridiculously fun. How can the world feel, momentarily, this good? She likes her nephew so much. He's loose and kind and just unpredictable enough.

He is her only sister Ljilja's only son, the single offspring of the family, and the focus of much attention. This unlikely Paris detour, on their way to visit his grandmother, Mira's mother, was his idea — a rather outrageous detour, given her mother's recent mini-stroke and the uncertain state of her health.

She wondered why he suggested this but was secretly thrilled — what a chance, among other things, to reconnect with him and enjoy the easy companionship they've shared since he was a tiny boy.

This time he is meeting some friends in Italy after Croatia, but last summer he was here with his ex-girlfriend Aisha. They texted Mira pictures of themselves in locations made deliberately unrecognizable: chain-link fence and grass behind their happy faces, extreme closeups of their chins above porcelain coffee cups — definitely no Arc de Triomph or even a hint of the recognizable massive buildings. This generation must be more ironic, she thought, looking at those pictures. How was it that things ended so badly with Aisha? But this was just one thing she wondered, which, she supposed, was really none of her business.

After Paris he and Aisha had gone on to Spain and Croatia, where they made a stop to see his grandmother — the grandmother he's spent many summers with, who instilled in him a love of dumplings and crepes, had helped make it so that, although he takes after his dad and looks mostly Chinese, he speaks Croatian as well as English.

They pass a group of men in front of a fruit shop, standing in a triangle near the angled crates of apples and peaches and oranges, smoking and talking; the marvel of how life goes on everywhere, all the time, all at once. One of them, a thin and dark-haired man, in an oversized beige wool cardigan, with lively wrists bending as he talks, reminds her of David.

About David, she always thinks: husband. Not *ex-husband*, even though they separated a couple of years ago already and the divorce has been final since last spring. She's not delusional; he's merely the only husband she's had. They happen rather a lot, these visions of him: sometimes it's just a messenger bag slung low over a hip, or the back of his head glimpsed through a coffee shop window.

Then, about to turn a corner, Bernard, still in front of her, nearly runs over a pigeon, a pigeon hanging out on the sidewalk, not doing the expected thing of flying away to avoid getting run over.

"Whoa, whoa," Bernard says.

She pedals ahead but he's not following, instead has dismounted and is watching the bird.

"He's hurt."

She backs up and dismounts too and leans over to look. One of the pigeon's wings hangs funny, like a part has come loose. What small parts do pigeons have under their feathers?

Bones, of course, get a grip. The pigeon stops fluttering, as if gathering strength, then tries to fly up. It reaches Bernard's knees and comes down. It pauses, longer this time. Flies up once more. Hovering at knee height a bit ahead of Bernard, it beats and beats and beats its wings and maybe it really can fly away. But no, it can't, it lands. And then it just huddles, like it knows. Doom.

"Poor thing," she says, getting her foot back on the bike.

"We need a box," Bernard says.

She looks up the street — Paris! — and the muscles in her legs, her whole body, wish to continue. Then looks down at the pigeon — could this random bird really form such an obstacle?

"What would you do with a box?"

Bernard is leaning over the bird, his hands on his knees. He looks up at her.

"Last summer I found a pigeon just like this, unable to fly, in the alley behind my and Aisha's old place."

"Right."

"I just left him there."

As if reading her silence, he says, "What else should I have done? Well, a pretty easy thing, Aisha said: get a shoe box, line it with some flyers, put the pigeon inside, give it a little water and bread, put him in a corner of the balcony, somewhere quiet and darkish, and let him be."

Sure, Mira thinks, Aisha would know. She knew how to handle small skittish creatures.

"But there must be dying pigeons all over the city."

She can tell she's inflecting her sentences as if they were questions, like some uncertain twenty-year-old. The point is, there are many pigeons needing saving, and should we fool ourselves that saving this one is going to change anything in the grand map of pigeon and other suffering?

"Instead, I left it there and an hour later I found it dead."

"We'd have to carry it back to the hotel, and what, ask for a box at reception?"

"No, if you stay here, I'll bike super fast and get a box somewhere."

"I'd rather do the biking, honest." Was she going to hang out on this sidewalk watching over a pigeon? She was too old to respectably sit on curbs.

"Oh, we passed that fruit shop!"

And so Bernard jogs off toward the now distant awning where the three men still stand talking.

Mira watches the pigeon, from a reasonable standing distance, sitting silently inside its pain. Then she checks her phone for any calls from Mom, then checks her email. She's waiting for an email, but then, everyone is always waiting for an email? No, she is really earnestly waiting for it, because here she is, already in Paris—and still, Mirko, that old ache, the other big reason she agreed to go to Paris, has not written yet. Nor called the number she wrote in her message to him. What can she do? She doesn't have his phone number, only that work email and a dubious home address, matching his surname and first initial, which may or may not be his.

Some years after their parting, at the farm where he tended bees with other men raw with what some people were calling PTSD, she heard that he'd moved to Paris. They'd lost touch by then, and she'd lost track of even his parents, so she couldn't ask them. So when Bernard suggested staying in Paris for a few days before catching a flight to Zagreb, she searched the internet for any mention, a picture, a scrap of context. What she found, as well as the potential home address, was a friendly and rudimentary website for a small roofing company, with a list of employees accompanied by tiny photos and email addresses. And she recognized Mirko, despite the photo being grainy and pixelated, and wrote to him: a carefully light and earnest message, which didn't mention their bitter parting.

She has a feeling he's not married. If he has children, it's a son or daughter living somewhere else with their mother, a person Mirko briefly loved. She doesn't know this, of course. But she thinks that if she showed up at his door, she would find him in a small flat of his own rather than a large one filled with children's backpacks and sneakers; she would find him encumbered, like her, mostly by the past. And since they are both middle-aged now, he may well be doing some soul-searching work himself, and welcome her — yes? The address is in the 14th arrondissement, with no huge attractions nearby, but still quite central. Close enough to her and Bernard's hotel that she could get there just by taking a long walk. Perhaps a rent-controlled place he's lived in for many years? Is there rent control in Paris?

Before she closes the browser now, she scrolls through the news captions on the Yahoo home page. The first is a video titled: "A race like no other: the 100-metre stiletto dash." Then, also, Israel is building 2000 new settlements in the West Bank. Further, you can "Look inside the mansion of the deposed president of Belarus." This last link blurb comes with a teaser: The mansion has twenty-three solid gold bidets. And the teaser subtitle asks: *Do you know what a bidet is really for?*

Mental note: remember to read real news later, read what is happening in the West Bank. As for stilettos, they are the devil's work: running in them, the women and one man look tense, greedy and vulnerable. Only one falls, the ankle caving in like bent rubber, while the winner cheers at the finish line, shaking her hot-shorts-with-the-stars-and stripes-clad-bum.

It is the first time she is travelling so well connected — for instance, with this data packet that lets her look at email on her phone. So Mirko has still not written, but oh, she just has to look into the distance beyond the striped fruit shop awning, and she knows that he is somewhere in this city, somewhere airy, somewhere with a window looking onto a sprightly courtyard; or somewhere dark, with grit in the air, and gritty neighbours; wherever he is, she feels the city like a big lung he draws air into and out of, a lung she has entered, which does not feel sturdy and reliably constructed, but capricious and heaving and fragile.

A couple of minutes later Bernard is running back with an empty cardboard fruit crate, pictures of oranges printed on its side. He takes off his jacket and picks up the pigeon — and after some struggle, some flapping, some shh, shhs from Bernard, it's wrapped safely inside his jacket. He carries this pigeon bundle against his chest while steering the bike with his other hand.

Mira carries the crate.

By the time they return the bikes at a bike station, walk to the hotel, climb the hotel stairs sheepishly with the hidden pigeon, settle the bird in a corner of Mira's room — why my room, she asks, but Bernard says, somewhat impatiently, it has a better corner; by the time they sneak downstairs and get a piece of baguette from the common kitchen and thieve a shallow butter dish for the pigeon's water; by the time they do all that, in her opinion quite illegally — because it can't be great for hygiene to have pigeons or other fowl around the hotel? — well, by then it's past lunchtime and they're starving.

The pigeon, however, does look the model of sad repose, all huddled and endearing.

They set out again, silent and a little cranky, and Bernard leads them on a now more vigorous ride, through the park behind the Louvre, through the Place de la Concorde, then on to the Champs-Élysées. He and Aisha must've hit these big landmarks after all, for him to know the way so well? The park alone dazzles her, with its wide graveled paths, and the landscape designed for width, for the eye surveying broadly; there are curves everywhere, in benches and flower plot fences — and then the flowers themselves, and the manicured bushes! And the people reclining elegantly on benches, alone or in pairs, some eating sandwiches out of white paper sleeves, others reading, legs crossed — such marvellous leisure!

Bernard seems to have a predetermined path. At a few intersections he merely hesitates briefly, and only in one place is he stuck for a while, choosing which way to continue.

And he won't take her advice on it, either. She doesn't know why it should matter — but the pauses, at least, give her a chance to snap some pictures with her phone.

They stop next to some statue of a man on a horse — there are so many statues! — for Bernard to take off his sweater. This is also the kind of twenty-three-year-old he is: he carries a backpack, to have room for a water bottle and sunscreen and a light sweater, just in case.

As a child he was skinny and brittle-seeming, but sometime in adolescence he transformed into an improbably tall and sturdy creature. What's stayed the same is his supernaturally translucent pale skin, and also his dark hair: straight and wispy, it falls around and into his eyes.

While he takes time rearranging the contents of his bag, she looks at the warrior on the horse. He's got flowing hair, waves down to his shoulders and a sword that hangs low and loose in his arm, its tip by his boot. The boot has a bow near the overturned top, as if it belonged to an illustration of the Puss in Boots fairy tale. What's with that hair and those boots, she thinks — just as she remembers a photograph, a photo of Aisha's winking face under that funny bow, the bow looking as if it's on top of her head, just the way people pose to make it seem that they're holding up the leaning tower of Pisa with their palm.

She checks her phone again, for any calls from Mom. There's a text from her sister, along with a selfie of her and Bernard's dad Dennis clinking gleaming glasses of white wine.

Well, how is it?? Bernard said you had to carry your suitcases up six flights of stairs. That's what you get for not staying in a normal hotel, haha. But seriously, remind him to watch his back. Haven't got a hold of mom today. I'll try to call tonight when it's morning over there.

This was the thing she and Ljilja had worried about: that Mom would some day end up ill and alone, and they'd have to fly back and forth to care for her. How much can one fly back and forth, what with an ordinary job and an ordinary salary? And who is to do the daily care: who can be trusted? And how much does it all cost?

And now that's precisely what's happening. Mira took an unpaid leave to make this trip without knowing what she would even accomplish in these three weeks. Or what she might do if things got worse — another stroke, a real stroke, a bad one? The thing hanging over her was if she should — ought to, really — find a way to move back there, take care of Mom, and just stop pretending she has some very important life, here or anywhere.

She wondered, how does a person ever decide where she ought to be?

Yet, at other points in her life, she had been sure where she should be. With David, for instance — that was easy, she should be where David is!

Well, no help that, now. Now, more concretely, she was looking into what kind of work she could possibly get in Croatia. She wasn't sure if she was looking into it to make it possible or to rule out the possibility. But in a neighbouring town an English-language school had opened up and an old acquaintance told her they'd be sure to take her. But, living with Mom and commuting — tricky. Living not so terribly far, as in another town, maybe possible? But also, becoming a teacher? Could she?

The future was a shapeless thing, a knotty property somewhere in the hills, without clear boundary lines. She didn't know what kind of dwelling it could support but felt some urgency to fence and landscape it.

Her real dwelling was a one-bedroom walk-up on the south side of the city near the university where she worked at the Registrar's Office. In the summer, by the evening, it heated up so much that tall candles she kept on a cupboard next to the kitchen table bent over like sad willows. Unable to cook or read, she was stuck for what to do — drive to a mall or café, just for the air conditioning, that's what people did. That or take a cold shower and lie on the couch in your underwear, with the blinds down and curtains drawn.

She'd just needed a shelter after the separation and this place was close to work and cute. It took a little while to discover that in the summer it was too hot and in the winter the heat often gave out. Now her rent has gone up a second time, and this time a rather stupid and unjustified amount. She got the note slipped under her door, the day before flying out, after she had already splurged on the Paris leg of the trip, of course.

They want us out, said the older woman across the hall from her, the one who wore her grey hair in a long braid and seemed to spend a lot of time at the public library, judging from Mira seeing her there every time she dropped in for five minutes about once a month. "Condos," the woman said simply, and walked ahead of Mira on the stairs. And for a moment Mira thought, like a sucker, I guess then I could just buy a condo in a place I already know.

In any case, her rent could now be a mortgage payment on a much more decent place, and she really felt pressure to get out of there: to act like an adult and not, as everyone put it, waste money on rent. Was rent really wasted? Well, in any case, every month, she saw the small sum she'd walked away from the divorce with sit quietly in her account, and now she would probably have to start dipping into it, diminishing it month by month. She also saw that between her and retirement there was not such a terribly long time and that her pension would not be amazing. And she has started to feel, deep in some primal fear centre, the need to cushion herself against those scary non-negotiables, like old age and death.

Yet the divorce — such a common adult thing to go through! — also made her feel like less of a grownup. She wondered, for instance, if she should, perhaps, go back to school? She had not managed to finish her degree during the war, but it hardly would've helped her in Canada, where she landed an office job only after she got a certificate in office administration. Her job at the Registrar's Office was fine, a middle-of-the-road job, one she could move up from into, say, a similarly administrative government job. But she had this extra time now — evenings and weekends that opened up like existential black holes — and should she put it toward some kind of self-reinvention?

"Ready to keep going?" says Bernard, looking a little askew in the collar area, his hair momentarily full of static, sweetly messy. Sometimes a sudden recollection of a child Bernard, just visible behind the adult, soft and playful, overwhelms her. It is less a recollection than an incarnation. She must look away to subdue it and keep going, neutral, as if not slayed by tenderness.

"How's your back?" she says, remembering Ljilja's worry. "You didn't aggravate that disc going up the stairs with your suitcase, did you?"

If she really moved back to Croatia, she'd be far from Bernard. And from Ljilja too, even though Ljilja and Dennis travelled so much now that she doesn't see them nearly as often as while she and David were married. To think that she and Ljilja had imagined Bernard and Aisha might be the ones getting married in a few years!

"Oh no," he says, "why is everyone so concerned about that?" He looks at his Android again, and puts it away, disappointed. He must be waiting for a message too.

Eventually they leave the bikes at a drop off point and walk the famous stretch of Champs-Élysées, looking for lunch. They pass cafés, cosmetics shops, clothes shops, the Dior store, a McDonald's. Groups of people, and aside from the obvious ones with cameras and open guidebooks, Mira can't tell who's a tourist and who goes for lunch on the Champs-Élysées on just any old Tuesday.

But not everyone is lunching. A short distance from the H&M clothing store a woman tries to catch the eyes of those who pass near her and to entreat them for change. A bit farther up, another beggar, this one curled up on the ground between the shops and the busy sidewalk.

A Roma woman, Mira guesses, though she can't see her face. She is sitting on her haunches, her back curled over her knees, her head covered with a scarf. Her forehead rests on the ground — on the actual concrete of the sidewalk. She has one arm tucked in and the other extended in supplication of alms. A McDonald's coffee cup next to her for coins.

Bernard stops.

The woman moves her other arm to adjust the scarf covering her head and is then again perfectly still.

"Jesus," he says.

Mira has seen, in Croatia, and other places in Europe, sad women like pietàs holding rag-wrapped, silent infants, and intoning supplications. But she too is struck by this prostrate creature and her perfect self-denigration. Humble, yet shameless, to put on such a show?

"Well. Do you mind if I step in there for some cheap shades?" He points to the H&M store. "I must have left my Ray-Bans on the plane."

She follows him in. It turns out that the Champs-Élysées H&M is not much more sophisticated than the West Edmonton Mall one: the racks are overfull, the sales piles treated with greed and contempt. Clothes are on the floor or half-hanging off hangers, tangled with one another; there is hose among t-shirts, collars pulled over someone's powdered face and left stained for someone else to consider. The sales staff fold or walk around looking put upon and important, but don't seem to improve the state of things. As for the shoppers, they range from skinny teens to middle-aged women with neck scarfs, like Mira.

She remembers boutiques where you did not disturb the saleswomen's folding because one of each item was hung for display. If you did pick anything up, you returned it slowly to its place, to not ire those women. You could not buy a thing and then just bring it back, linty and smelling like your own house, and expect to get your money back. Clothes with defects were not sold, ever. Look at this, for instance — a pretty flower-patterned blouse, but a smear of blush along the inside of the collar, two buttons loose, and a long thread hanging from the sleeve. Acrylic, made in Cambodia, on sale for twelve euros. But for that price maybe she could tidy it up?

There was Bernard, trying on pair after pair of sunglasses, attempting to see his face in the narrow mirror of the sunglass rack, calmly ignoring those flittering about him, looking at home in this environment. But it must not be a generational thing; anyone can get into the spirit of things. People have engaged in less-than-dignified commerce for centuries, haven't they? Look at her, digging now through the neckerchiefs and pulling out one that would do just fine, is just what she needs, a soft pale yellow and not silk but nonetheless with a fine feel, reduced to nine euros.

It makes this depressing business worthwhile, she thinks, in line to pay, thank God, the last humiliating step.

From a corner of the store, a hulking man in a suit, and with one of those ear and mouth pieces that always make her picture Madonna performing "Vogue," is looking at her.

Stuffing the now-paid-for scarf into her purse, wondering if she'd been earmarked as a potential thief, she calls to Bernard, in Croatian, across a rack of pink animal-print cargo pants. Somehow here they speak Croatian more, as if they don't want to be like so many other English-speaking tourists.

Bernard walks over to stand in front of her, wearing large, funny sunglasses.

"Just tell me — these?"

She really wants to get out of here, but she hates to lie to him, so she says, "No, I don't think so. The white frame is a little — cartoonish? Too *street*? Too faux-hip?"

Suddenly, the large man appears beside them.

"You too are from the old country," he says, grinning.

Up close, there is no mistaking his face; it immediately puts her in mind of family barbecues from her childhood, the neighbouring men roasting sausages in her parents' yard.

"I heard you yelling across the store and I like to hear our language in this foreignness. You live in Paris?"

"We are passing through, sort of," she says, turning toward Bernard so as to include him, though he has returned to his sunglasses and only sends a smile their way. He smiles too much, she thinks.

"We are on our way home, to visit, from Canada."

"Canada! I have an uncle there, in Scarborough. You been abroad for long?"

"Nearly twenty years."

Ex-Yugos in foreign places like to get familiar quickly, but since the war they also have some reserve. Yet she hardly feels any reserve at all, because, in fact, he looks rather like Mirko: a thick brow, almost like a canopy over his eyes, and the same upper lip, with a slight overbite.

The similarity is both disturbing and a comfort, the way when you're waiting for a bus even the wrong ones will reassure you that you're not entirely in the wrong place, somewhere no bus could ever be expected to stop.

But, of course, a man who looks like Mirko makes the real Mirko no more or less likely to appear.

He gestures with his finger to say, just a moment, and speaks into his mouthpiece in French, clunky but earnest French, slowly enunciated, not arrogantly thrown around: it is the way her dad spoke English, with David, for instance, when he wished to be polite. This man is not as old as her father would be if he were alive; only, probably, a little too old to feel comfortable hulking over women shoppers who may be stealing hose or tank tops.

"Sorry about that. Coming up eighteen for me."

Eighteen years. Soon after the end of the war.

As if he's been talking to them all along, Bernard turns away from the mirror and says, "What is a good place to get

Balkan food in Paris?" He knows he speaks an Anglo-inflected Croatian, with rounded *a*s and *o*s, and thick *t*s, all wanting to be *th* sounds. But he's hardly ever shy or reluctant to talk, a confidence she both admires and envies.

"Did I say that right?" he says now.

"You speak terrific! You were born abroad? The important thing is you are trying." The man pats Bernard's shoulder gently, encouragingly.

"There is a very good place on Rue du Simplon — Rue du Simplon," he repeats with slow enunciation, "a bit out of the way but easy to get to —" and here he searches his pockets, finds a receipt that he first studies then turns over and smooths out, and then slowly writes the metro line, the name of the stop, the number of the exit, and a diagram of the streets leading to the restaurant.

Bernard encourages him with nods and questions, but Mira cannot tell why on earth they would take the trouble, since they will have all the so-called Balkan food they want in a few days.

The man hands Bernard the paper, saying, "Are you seeing other things around here?"

But before Bernard can answer, the man is interrupted by another message coming through his headset. When he turns back to them, he speaks more quickly.

"I have gone to all the museums and the monuments. But the place you really must go to is Versailles, the Palace, if you have even a day to spare —"

"How far out of Paris is it?"

Another headset message, and an impatient response, Oui, oui, un moment.

"All of Paris is beautiful of course, except that it's getting destroyed by immigrants—"

And here the conversation makes astonishingly quick leaps from impressive monuments to clean streets to dirty streets to the immigrant problem.

"You must have noticed. Just too many people—one person gets their papers, but then they bring over a horde of elders and children. Half of them end up on social assistance. You see them in parks sometimes, smoking and looking listless, lazy. I mean that's the good side. The other is the crime. My mother visited, you know, I thought I could get her in as a cleaner somewhere, but do you know what happened?"—here his tone heightens—"The second day she was here she was mugged on the street—the tip of a knife above her elbow, and the punk ran off with her purse. The shame of it—a seventy-year-old woman."

Mira can see this being a story oft-repeated, a story made to represent all that is wrong with Paris. She might have expected this. She cannot recall seeing any gloomy groupings of elders and children in parks. But street cleaners from Africa, North Africa, sub-Saharan Africa, yes—ditto maids.

"So you too, an immigrant, tried to bring your mother over," says Bernard, icily, definitely not smiling anymore, only mangling the Croatian enough that the man seems uncertain of what's been said. "I'm going to go pay for my sunglasses."

Silence hangs between Mira and the man, only static coming through his headset.

He pulls out a business card from his shirt pocket.

"Here," he says, dropping his voice. "Call me sometime, while you're here. Doesn't matter when. I work late but I stay up late."

She takes the card and he straightens his posture, steps back a little.

"I'm always up," he says.

She walks out without looking at him and flicks the card onto the ground. She feels the prickles of adrenaline inside her and imagines walking back inside with the card and stuffing it in his mouth, pushing the edges against his gums. But why are her violent thoughts always so cartoonish? Why can't she have put him in his place with a few sharp words instead?

"What an ignoramus," Bernard says, behind her now on the street. "We should report him to the management."

"Indeed." And she puts on her sunglasses to hide the inexplicable welling up of her eyes. But it's not really inexplicable, just, maybe, pathetic. It's that every time she thinks someone might be a decent man to spend some time with, she finds not a crack of imperfection but a crater of folly.

They've walked a block and her heart has slowed down its fast thumping, when a man passes them on a bicycle, steering with one hand and with the other holding a cell phone into which he is nodding vigorously. David again. David nodded that much and was likely to steer one-handed. And for a moment, she's not sure it isn't actually him, that he's not come to Paris for some reason or another. A reunion!

If he saw her, he'd be kind. He'd forgiven her; they'd forgiven each other. In fact, seeing each other since the divorce, they are likely to be painfully considerate, and apologetic: as if the reality of the divorce has made them frightened and embarrassed of what they — of their own volition — have done to each other.

Though lately, she thinks, did they know what they were talking about when they doled out their forgiveness? Where does absolution come from?

BERNARD FINDS A table on a restaurant patio by the sidewalk. On a bench opposite the patio sits the same woman they'd seen kneeling on the ground. Now she's eating a sandwich; her headscarf is loosened, and beneath it are thick dark hair and a healthy-looking face. It's the headscarf that makes him sure it's the same woman.

"In China, apparently," he says to Mira now, putting down his macchiato, "the beggar is like a character type — a role, you know — and beggars have to look like beggars. Everyone says they're professionals. Which seems to me like just a way of making it seem that being destitute is as ordinary as being a dentist."

He remembers the beggars he saw in Suzhou, two summers ago, visiting east Asia for the first time with his dad. They sat at a table in front of a waffle-and-bubble-tea shop, when a very old man with a long, sparse squiggle of a grey beard, in a black robe both dirty and shiny from wear, leaning his bent form on a gnarly cane, walked up to them and rattled his coin cup. He said something in a high, entreating, disconcerting tone, which even Bernard's dad, though Mandarin was his mother tongue, did not quite get. Bernard was ashamed of himself for it, but he wished nothing more than to be out of the man's presence. Later, on the comfy seats of their tour bus, their youngish, confident guide, said, "There is no homelessness in China. That man you saw" — for everyone on the tour bus had seen him — "is a beggar by profession. Sometimes we joke they make as much money as tour guides!" Instead of joining the chuckling, Bernard simply looked out his window, at the fantastically large, elevated freeway they were driving on, its twelve lanes of traffic full, despite what they were told was a huge tax on owning an automobile.

The trouble in China was, he looked Chinese enough that people in, for instance, Shanghai thought he spoke Mandarin, and he realized just how much he didn't speak it. He felt oddly embarrassed, disappointing so many people who took him for one of their own: as if he were faking something with his looks. But how could it be his fault?

In Suzhou, the canals and bridges were beautiful, and the streets charming, lined with small eateries and shops, quirky, urban yet folksy, staffed by smiling, stylish young people with oversize-framed eyeglasses. But by the time they walked for several hours and were sitting down to bubble tea, and the beggar had come and gone, Bernard was suddenly suspicious: had he mistaken, say, one of those Ukrainian village recreations for an authentic, living place?

Why is everything everywhere always becoming a caricature of itself?

The thing about this woman, the woman on the bench he's staring at while trying not to be caught staring, is that her face, unmistakably, echoes Aisha's, and he is trying to pinpoint the similarity, as if looking for a word rolling around in his mouth.

Their sandwiches arrive, and they are decently sized if not generous, the coffee excellent, and the bill, which the waiter puts down along with the food, high. He expected all this, because he'd eaten here last summer with Aisha. They had a long and exuberant walk over here, but while they waited for their sandwiches, they argued. Why had he convinced her to wear the blue leather flats over her Birkenstocks? It was intrusive and unkind of him, she said. She knew they'd hurt her feet in the long run and told him as much. And now she was getting a blister that would bother her the whole rest of their trip. Was she saying he'd ruined their trip by making a suggestion about shoes? It was more than a suggestion, she said. He was embarrassed by her Birkenstocks, and that was shitty. Well, it's crazy to wear a beautiful dress — he'd pointed to it — and ruin it with ugly Birkenstocks. Seriously, she said? I'm sorry, I was an idiot, I feel terrible, he said, suddenly genuinely ashamed. I didn't think we'd walk so much.

He really didn't. It really was shitty, he added. But the other day you vetoed my band shirt! That's different, she said! She smacked the table with her palm; she often smacked something with the flat of her palm when she was angry. It's offensive! You can't walk around with an implicit image of breasts on your shirt!

On it went. He still thought the breasts she saw in that shirt were a fiction, but he felt bad about that fight, and especially about the blister, which really did hurt her for days.

There was a lot to feel bad about. But that was his purpose in Paris: to trace all the places he and Aisha spent time in and, by remembering — with the benefit of hindsight, of knowing what he now knows — to uncover what happened. To understand why he treated Aisha the way he did and why she left him the way she did. It's not a perfect plan. A compulsion more than a plan? But look — here he is, at the same restaurant, and a woman who looks like Aisha is sitting on a bench right across from him. It must mean something.

They eat quickly, as if making up for missed meals. Two women, at a table near theirs, are speaking Bosnian, not registering Bernard or Mira as people who might understand them.

Both women wear what looks to Bernard like expensive blazers and the kind of sleek leather purses Aisha admired but never splurged on; they are much older than him, but the one with the greying black hair pulled into a high ponytail is actually quite attractive. They are talking, it seems, about an affair one of them is in the middle of.

"Sometimes I'm driving home," says the ponytail one, "and my cell phone will ring — and I think, the jig is up. She looked at his phone while he was shaving or something, found the pathway to the secret texts. And then I think, thank God. Let it just be over, God. Come what may."

Jesus, Bernard thinks. Is that what Aisha thought — let it all come out, come what may?

"You are frayed," the friend says to the ponytail woman, looking keen and sympathetic, shaking a cigarette out of its pack, offering it to her friend.

"It would be ironic to get religious now, wouldn't it, rather than during the war."

They laugh gleefully at this, continue laughing when a waiter comes by and lowers their cappuccinos onto the table.

"Seriously?" Bernard says to Mira quietly, frowning, when they've finished their sandwiches. "Are there this many ex-Yugos in Paris?"

Mira says nothing but puts her sunglasses back on and takes a sip of her coffee.

But, in fact, she's lifting the empty cup in a mere gesture of drinking.

"I'm going inside to pay," she says.

He watches her disappear inside the wide door of the café, and he looks again at the girl still sitting on the bench. Girl, woman, how is he to know? In any case, she's come to the nub of her sandwich, the part that is probably just dry bread. Sitting there, she doesn't look ingratiating, nor humble; not proud, either, and not happy. When two pigeons land near her, she tosses them her last hunk of bread without looking their way.

Her head is now in almost perfect profile. Though she is far, he can see the shape of two very gentle slopes: the bridge, the tip — it's Aisha's nose.

This is as happy, as painful, a memory as any he has: sitting at the table in his grandmother's kitchen, his grandma to his right, and Aisha in perfect profile to his left. All of them snipping stems off roses they'd just cut from the huge rose patch at the back of the house. If a piece of stem landed on the floor, his grandma immediately picked it up and piled it on the table with the others. He could see her watching the way they worked and knew from the slight movement of her mouth when the cuts were too jerky and imprecise for her liking. Then he noticed a smudge of dirt on Aisha's jaw — she had taken off the garden gloves to feel the soil earlier — and when he motioned to point it out, Aisha swiped at it with her dirty forearm, and gave herself a whole dirty cheek.

Everyone laughed.

"Ah, so what," said his grandma, surprising Bernard, "a bit of dirt!"

Across the table, she watched Aisha with a look that was as close as she came to affection and approval — that despite the imprecise cutting and the needless soil poking. It was a look directed often at him, but not so often, as he has just recently realized, at many others.

His palms are sweaty. This Paris day is heating up furiously after an overcast morning.

That's how things were just that short while ago: his grandmother was well, and he and Aisha were happy. Mostly happy. And everyone had loved Aisha the way tight families do — protectively and with ever the slightest touch of force.

Now, his grandma will only say, when they phone each other, *That one.* As if Aisha deserved to be made generic, returned to her place among the contemptuous masses. To cast her out, they had to un-know her. His grandma never again tried to, the way she used to, wrap her mouth around the name, playing with the sound between the *a* and the *sh*, wishing to say it right. Last summer after their three-day visit, she was even inflecting Aisha's name in address, the way one does in Croatian: Ajšo moja, she said in parting, before taking Aisha's face between her hands to kiss it.

But *my Aisha* was no more. And even Mira, once her biggest fan, seemed to harden, just perceptibly, at the mention of her. His failure, surely, that he told them about the affair and let them think everything was Aisha's fault. Of course, at first, he felt he deserved all the sympathy! But it wasn't fair, it wasn't fair, and it seemed like one more slight against her that she would forever be the villain in his family's mind.

The girl brushes crumbs off her skirt, rises from the bench and turns her head in Bernard's direction. A measuring look, a questioning look, perhaps on just this side of contemptuous. It is not a look you answer with a smile, and for once, he doesn't. What can he do but hold her eyes, until she turns and walks away. In a moment she is just a scrap in the crowd, unreachable. Where must she walk to? She is replaced by Mira, approaching the table, almost rubbing shoulders with the Bosnian women, who have finished their coffees and are walking away.

ON THEIR WAY up the curving stairs of the hotel, on the first-floor landing, a maid pulls aside an unreasonably large vacuum cleaner to let them pass. The woman is Black, youngish, in a stiff grey dress, probably provided by some work uniform company, paid for out of her own pocket? How could she possibly get that monster vacuum up the stairs, Mira wonders? Maybe she vacuums only the hallways, sweeps the stairs with a broom? But the stairs too are carpeted. How to ask without looking like an idly curious dolt?

The woman does not acknowledge them. After Mira moved to Canada, when she was tentative about her English, she too had cleaned hotels, and rarely bothered looking up at people coming in and out of rooms. What for? They might as well have been sitcom characters from cable television, with their generic English names that she heard called out in the hallways. Standing at the ice machines in their boxer briefs, filling plastic buckets with ice cubes. She couldn't understand the endless need for ice, buckets of ice in the middle of winter. And in any case, she had to look down more than up — that's where the dirt, the refuse, inevitably collected.

"That dude was right," Bernard says, as they continue up the stairs, "the immigrants are having a ball here. Probably making a killing. Probably supporting an extended family of twenty on that awesome maid wage."

Now on the third floor, they pass a just-vacated room, its door fully ajar. They both look inside. Any open door, any curtain not drawn in the evening, and one will look. Another maid, this one decidedly young, is running a grey rag over the bed's headboard, and she does link eyes with them when she sees them in the doorway — she smiles faintly, as if to say, I get it, I'd look in too. You can only stay in one room at a time, and so many others exist, and what are they like?

Bernard chose the hotel and Mira hadn't thought to ask about it. And when it turned out, upon arrival this morning, that he got the very same room he stayed in with Aisha, last August, before the small fiasco of their breakup, Mira offered to switch rooms with him. He quickly agreed.

She has carried him around smooshed into what they called "a little ball of child" when he was a skinny three-year-old, squeaky with happiness, a boy yelling, Make me into a smaller ball, aunty, smaller! This as she pushed gently on his head with one hand and cradled his little spine with the other, pretending to work hard at balling him up. That was joy. So she couldn't scold him now, couldn't say — what were you thinking choosing the same hotel in the first place?

It's a fine hotel, central, not cheap but not terribly expensive, good enough for the three nights before they catch their flight to Croatia. All the people working here, other than the owners, seem to be — what, immigrants, refugees, foreign workers? As they waited at reception while the hurried owner, his hair like tufts of white cotton candy, looked for their names on the list of reservations, she could see a man pushing a length of wire down the drain of a sink in a small bathroom in the hallway — a Slavic man, surely; these maids — Ethiopian? But what does she know. What can you tell just by looking at a person, and that in a strange place like Paris?

It's a one-star hotel but includes a breakfast of coffee, baguette, processed cheese triangles, Nutella, butter, jam, and canned fruit salad. Charming dining room right next to the entrance way, scallop-edge curtains, wooden chairs with round backs, cute red trays the baguette, etc., arrives on. Coffee not bad. Old Paris building so no elevator, just those winding narrow stairs — nothing to mind about that, once you've got your luggage to the sixth floor, where their rooms are, across the hall from each other. They got the medium-cheap rooms — in-suite toilet in a tiny cubicle, but shared shower down the hall for the whole floor. This a little icky, other people's hair in drains, fungus potential, but, still, fine, ten minutes a day in a shower, wear flip-flops, not a big deal.

She is glad to be back here after the unsettling lunch. She's not gone home in two years, since her dad's funeral, and these hints of home, the security guard, the Bosnian women, are the vague door knocks of a night dream, insistent tapping of unspecified meaning.

When they've finally made it to the sixth floor, to her room, which should've been Bernard's, they hunch over the pigeon in its fruit box. It's alive, sitting still in a corner, and the crumbs strewn around show it has eaten some bread. Bernard crumbles in more bread from the piece of baguette he saved from lunch, and then he opens a bottle of wine he bought along the way — he's got an opener in his jacket pocket. He pours wine into a plastic cup from the bathroom and goes to stand by the balcony door, looks at the room from that angle. Then he opens her closet — empty, because three days is no time to unpack for.

"Same smell," he says, with his head inside it. "Slightly damp, slightly stale wood."

She thinks, he must have hung his own shirts in that damp wooden closet. What strange behaviour, smelling the wardrobe, looking down on the same view from the balcony. Was it because he was still heartbroken? Think of all the relationships ahead of you, she wanted to say to him! Do you even know how young you are?

But then, she wasn't sure that was true, that he was all that young. Did she not overestimate the duration of her own youth?

Then he sits down on the bed, puts his feet up, props up his back with pillows.

He has another plastic cup ready for her, but she declines; since the divorce, she almost never drinks.

He runs his hand along the bedspread, smoothed out by the maid.

"Holy shit, this stain! Look!"

"Where?"

"This patch, see this outline?" He points to a faint outline of dark orange on the dark-orangish bedspread. She leans in over the wing of the armchair where she's sitting.

"Wine spill?"

"Aisha spilled that wine! We were always drinking wine on the bed and looking at the guidebook. Wow. Still there. Same bedding."

One star indeed.

She leans back into the armchair, tells herself: hostility is an unproductive emotion. Don't hate Aisha. Aisha was just a baby. What did you know at twenty-four? How many hearts did you betray, on both continents, getting seduced by bartenders, middle-aged poets, hell, the night nurse at the hospital while waiting for Dad's appendix surgery, then that really rather unkempt but strangely — well, better not to go down that list. Focus instead on Bernard, on Aisha, not knowing better.

He makes a sucking noise with his mouth, which his grandpa used to make, when he was nervous or worried or supressing displeasure. She looks at Bernard more closely, to see if the pose of easy rest, legs crossed at the ankles, is actually a front.

Then his phone chimes, and he thumbs a message. One thing about people immersed in their devices: they're un-selfconscious, their faces spontaneously radiating emotion.

It's like looking in on someone through a window, in their private moment, as they're beaming over their firstborn in its crib.

"I don't mean to pry," she says, "but — who are you texting with?"

She should not speak this way, but something about the whole day — maybe the pigeon, maybe the now-ugly-looking scarf she's bought? — is making her feel not fully in control.

"Ha ha, you don't mean to pry. Like no one in our family ever pries, right. Actually, I wanted to tell Aisha about the room — I mean the same room, the stain — it's too much of a coincidence. Isn't it?"

Bernard is not private, not exactly shy, although he's capable of mysterious shifts and unexpected sensitivity. She knew him to be this way since his childhood, when she and David spent occasional weekends with him. During several sleepovers, he'd wake up again and again and each time pick up the same sad cry for Mom and Dad: as if the wail for home were eternal and unceasing and sleep only a brief distraction. *Inconsolable,* she thought then, a word she'd never used before.

Why did we insist on those sleepovers with the poor kid, she wonders now?

"I don't mean this unkindly," she says, "but have you heard expressions like, don't pick a scab? Don't finger the wound? Don't run your tongue over the tooth hole?"

"Your tongue over the tooth hole? Really?"

"Fine. Those are not exactly proverbs. But still—"

"I also had to tell her about the Roma girl. Because that girl looked so much like her. Isn't that wild? I knew she'd like to hear that."

"I guess she did look like her? I didn't really catch it."

But the girl did have the heart-shaped face, small mouth and large eyes of Aisha. The repetition of this facial combination must not be uncanny — merely a manifestation of some unknown-to-her principles of human genetic connectedness. But it made her uncomfortable. She had liked Aisha so much. All the worse, now: more disappointment.

What wasn't disappointing? Like that security guard, at first so warm and familiar.

And would Aisha like to hear about the resemblance, since, truth be told, her family had been painfully poor, Aisha's schooling funded solely by ridiculously good grades and student loans? You might not get a kick out of being compared to a panhandler, in that case?

"Aisha said, I guess one could be a beggar in worse places than the Champs-Élysées."

Yeah, right, Mira thinks.

He puts his phone down, makes that sucking noise with his lip again. "I know you all think she's to blame for everything."

True. She just has to think back to Bernard weeping first in her living room, and then again at his parents' place. Mira wondered if he ever regretted telling them what he'd found out and then dealing with all their indignation. We let her in!

45

We trusted her! Ljilja exclaimed, as if they were the ones Aisha had left.

They also thought Bernard still held out hope, which all of them — Bernard's parents, heck, even grandparents, all feeling personally betrayed, thought was their job to sack. We have to nip that shit in the bud, Ljilja said, it's a done deal, no way that girl's coming back. Once a cheater, always a — Bernard's dad tried to pipe in, but Ljilja cut him off with, Don't pull out the clichés, would you, this is our son we're talking about, our first-and-only-born!

Collectively, then, they were supposed to be part of the same Project No Hope; they were supposed to have excised Aisha like a suspicious lump — so what was Mira doing now, participating in all this reminiscing? Even now, for instance, Bernard was looking around the room in that intense way, as if he were peering through a magic device, a time-travel telescope that showed reels from the past superbly more vivid and meaningful than the present.

He swishes wine in his mouth. His skin has the faintest blush along the neck and cheeks, pale gentle redness you see in the flesh of some apples when you slice them open.

"I wish you wouldn't," he says, mouth pursed. "Blame her. You don't know how I can get. Our family never talks about relevant things."

She could say, I do know you, I've known you since before you knew yourself, and when you were a kid, you'd look exactly like this, obstinate and vulnerable and on the edge of something, seesawing. She could say, What family does talk about relevant things?

"I wasn't always pleasant to be around. I stifled her."

This too he had as a child, the same tone of trust and straightforwardness: "This girl took my pencil, and I said, give it back because my grandma gave it to me, and she said, no, it's her pencil, and why, why would she do that?" Every such story pinched Mira's heart with worry and terrible softness.

He doesn't look at her. But stifled is neither here nor there, is it?

"Maybe I'm old-fashioned, but that's no reason to have an affair —"

"Right."

"I didn't mean that so judgmentally."

"I never wanted her to leave."

"You loved her."

He runs his fingertips over the wine stain on the duvet, gently and rhythmically, such that a part of her wishes to tell him he doesn't need to explain, it's fine, it was what it was, and another part wishes that whatever is compelling him to speak this way will persist until he has explained everything, and she can't wait to hear.

"I hate people like that guy at the store," he says. "So entitled, and mean, under that comradely bullshit."

"That guy? There's a million idiots like him around."

"Like what the fuck's he doing here? He's God's gift to France?"

There is some rustling in the pigeon box — the words "Finest Navel Oranges" printed on its side — and Bernard rises from the bed. He crouches by the box again, reaches out but then withdraws his hand.

She leans forward in the armchair. "Do you think that wing might heal?"

"It might. I have no idea. I don't know anything about pigeons."

He stands up quickly.

"Well, thanks," he says.

And just like that, he leaves the room.

Did she say something stupid? What has she said?

Though, really, why is he so sensitive? What has been so hard about his life?

In his later adolescence she had tuned out, a little, what with her own mess of a life. But during her prolonged separation, when she finally moved into her own place, her apartment was within walking distance from campus, and Bernard, who was doing his Bachelor of Science by then, would sometimes stop in for a late afternoon beer or a veggie burger.

Soon he started bringing Aisha along, and then there they'd be, at her door, Mira grateful for the company and nearly in awe that they would grant it. They'd bring ingredients for veggie samosas or some other thing Aisha was so good at making. Aisha warm and practical, quickly finding her way in the humble kitchen, unfazed by yesterday's unwashed dishes; Bernard smitten, eager to please Aisha, checking if he's folding the dough correctly and mincing the garlic finely enough. In those early days of their relationship, they both still lived at home, and Mira soon gave them her keys. Then she might come home from work and find Aisha napping on her bed, waiting for Bernard to finish his night class.

"You're like a man," Mira said to her once. "You can fall asleep in an instant."

"Only some places. Here I feel good. Also, I wake up in the night and then I study. Like, I can't stop thinking about school and then I just get up and read my textbooks. Could I take a shower, aunty?"

Mira couldn't tell if Aisha seemed young or old for her age. She seemed motherly in her cooking and her insistence Bernard eat homemade food rather than nachos at the campus bar. But she also had manners with Mira that seemed like those of a well-behaved teenager. She'd text Mira to tell her they both made it home if they left late. Her seriousness about school had the earnestness of someone trained to be a good pupil, yet there was also her savviness about scholarships and connections with professors, which struck Mira as responsible and smart, and even, occasionally, verging on cunning. And she understood perfectly how her student loans worked and how to apply for references, which was more than could be said of Bernard.

When they were moving in together, Aisha dealt with the landlords and read the rental agreement. By then, being ahead of Bernard in school, she was starting a master's degree in animal science. Bernard had quit vegetarianism and she and Bernard ate a lot of chicken: perfectly healthy chicken bred for research, officially forbidden but quietly snuck out by all the grad students — many of them poor, some raising kids on grad student funding. Aisha wanted to become, eventually, a large-animal veterinarian — horses, cows, pigs — which were scarce, such veterinarians, everyone opting for smaller, cuter animals.

Admirable, this, like so many things about Aisha. It was thus more shocking to learn of her affair with another animal scientist, a poultry expert whom she now loves — though maybe she still loves Bernard, from what Mira has gathered through Ljilja, through Bernard's one or two hints? And really too bad, really very hurtful, for Bernard to have found out the way he did, young people these days being so strangely keen on documenting in digital form all their mischief.

Bernard was the one to tell Mira about the pictures and videos he found. There was a dinner outing planned that night with Ljilja and Dennis and Mira — she was the pity guest, she felt, but she'd take the pity — and Bernard and Aisha and Aisha's mom, but about an hour before, Bernard buzzed her door. He smelled faintly of weed and his skin had the hanging look of someone who hasn't slept.

"We can't have dinner tonight," he said. "Aisha left me." She remembers how he said it almost meanly, as if blaming her.

"It can't be!"

"It's true. She's got someone else!" He yelled at her, yes, he did. And then he was sitting on the couch and telling her how he found Aisha's phone, saw the pictures, confronted her, and later that night went to sleep at a friend's place, where he's been for the last two days.

Even that night, she remembers, he left like this, with no warning, closing off suddenly.

Well. Maybe it's for the better he's gone now. She should probably worry less about Bernard and more about her mother. She's the one alone, the one who, increasingly, sounds anxious whenever they talk. When Mira talked to her on the phone the night before she and Bernard flew out, her voice came faint and broken up by shallow breaths.

"Are you coming?" she'd said. "Is Bernard coming?"

Then more laborious breathing. This woman, Mira's mother, blessed until recently with seemingly perfect health, has always treated physical infirmity with suspicion, as if it were willed more than actual. When Mira broke her ankle in grade six at school, her mother didn't seem to believe her, as if she couldn't imagine a hardy twelve-year-old could be so easily crippled.

"What did you do?" she'd said to Mira with a sceptical furrow to her brow, sitting in a kitchen chair across from her, after Mira managed to take off her sneaker. She'd walked home from school and the swelling had made her shoe very tight.

"I was just walking down the stairs."

"Had they just been washed or something?"

She leaned down and took Mira's heel in the palm of her hand for a second and then quickly let it go and sat back. The slight grimace meant Mira's foot wasn't perfectly clean.

Her dad, clipping on his wristwatch, appeared in the doorway.

"I'm off," he said. He nodded toward the foot, which meant, what is that all about?

"She says she was just walking down the stairs."

"That looks like a lot of swelling to me. I'd take her to the clinic." He shook out his shirt collar, as was his habit, and walked toward the hallway. "I won't be out long. Make them give her a cast if she needs it," he called out, right before the door closed behind him.

Mira remembers how her mother's mood darkened. Such shifts Mira registered as unambiguously as if they were bells ringing, and she knew that, as usual, it didn't bode well for her.

"Well, we're going to the clinic then. I suppose he took the car. We better get that shoe back on somehow."

While she was walking, she didn't cry, because crying in the middle of the street would not do, would make her mother angry — what a scene it would be! And then how embarrassed she was to sob, as soon as she had sat down in the full waiting room. Somehow it spilled out of her, and once it did, she couldn't stop it — as if she'd momentarily lost a grip on a rock she'd been holding in her palm, and then could do nothing but watch it bump loudly all the way down the hill. So she'd made a scene after all.

"You're not a little child," her mom said, quietly, not looking at her.

And really, she thought much later, maybe she remembers all of that because some squishy child part of her twelve-year-old body did harden.

And every now and then, after much walking, or on a day spent in uncomfortable shoes, her ankle will throb, faintly, familiarly, in her tibia, a gentle echo of that long-ago pain.

But, her mother. She herself had never broken a bone, never suffered headaches or back pain like everyone else. She rode her bicycle everywhere and did Jane Fonda videos at home, on the living room carpet, when not a single person they knew did that. And she hardly ever came down with colds, which she believed was due to her careful diet and propolis supplements, and also her impeccable hygiene. Demented hygiene, Mira thought. Could sheets left on a bed for more than three days do grave damage? If you brushed your teeth six times a day, wasn't there some law of diminishing returns? But since mom's mini-stroke a month ago she's shown less of her usual hardiness.

"Is Ljilja coming?" Mom asked that last time on the phone, once she'd got her breath back.

But Ljilja, along with Bernard's dad Dennis, was on Vancouver Island. Their West Coast jaunts have become a habit: Ljilja became a real estate agent some years back, and they'd got themselves a small place in North Saanich. Mira thought of her sister as practical, and brave. She and Dennis went out to the Island and San Francisco and Hawaii for fun, as if they were retired, which they weren't; they'd only arranged things to suit themselves.

That was the brave thing — arranging matters to suit yourself, which might have been a survival thing. At some point during Dennis's long depressive period that stretched through much of Bernard's childhood, Ljilja said: enough. If we're going to live rather than die, then we have to live on our own terms.

She wasn't the depressed one, but she was not well, either. One day while Mira was over, Ljilja stepped on the lens of Bernard's toy microscope and, after yelling, Fuck, fuck, fuck!, she threw the broken pieces against the wall, then ran into Bernard's room and grabbed the microscope, one-handed, and, as if she were throwing a baseball, launched it at the window. The slats of a partially pulled down blind twisted and the glass cracked. Okay, okay, okay, Mira said, at a reasonable distance, as Ljilja sat on the floor and wept.

She announced, shortly after, We're just going to do exactly what we like doing. You feel better by the ocean, Dennis? Okay. I like the ocean. We'll get to the ocean. Of course, they still had a mortgage. But somehow, they found the money. We're making tradeoffs, Ljilja said. So Bernard will have to pay for university. That's alright. He'll find his own way to live!

But maybe even more than raiding Bernard's university fund or finding a way to go snorkeling every afternoon, the striking thing to Mira was how they stopped pleasing both other people and real or imagined gods.

When Mom collapsed and went into the hospital, they'd already had their time on the coast booked.

"It's better if we visit in shifts," Ljilja said, which seemed true enough. Bernard, who'd graduated last winter and was starting a master's degree in the fall, had a trip to Italy planned with a couple of friends and he'd only be staying in Croatia for a few days. So Mira arranged her unpaid leave, vaguely worrying if it would put her on the unfavourables list of her new boss, and tagged along with Bernard, and while Ljilja and Dennis flew west, onto the shores of the Pacific, she and Bernard flew east across the Atlantic.

AFTER BERNARD LEAVES, Mira neither calls nor texts her mom. It's because she actually wants, instead, to sleep, to sleep all the way to dawn. But it's not tomorrow she wants, so much as a whole other day — a day not before or after, but a parallel one: this one, revised. She continues to sit in the armchair, staring out at the balcony railing, at the mute, early-evening light of a city not her own.

She can't really sleep. Instead, before she knows it, she starts going down the list of all her own old disappointments. This brooding happens a lot lately, a most unattractive habit, as powerful, indeed, as the heaviest narcotics-induced sleep. Her head drops over the back of the armchair and her breathing slows. The list is bitter, yes, but also punctuated with pokes of painful affection for its protagonists, those misbehavers and insufficients. David, of course, who left so abruptly, went far, overseas, and, although he said he was willing to talk about the marriage, he could only do that over a crackly internet phone line, filled with echo from his cheap cell phone and obscured by the wind. Why is there always wind, she had cried once, after answering the phone and hearing yet again the crinkle and hollow swoosh where her husband should have been. Baffled, despairing of her inability to interpret yet another persistent pattern. Could he not have phoned from a café, at least?

But who is she to speak of betrayals, David's or Aisha's or anyone's? Her own are just another long list. *It's just that you didn't even see me for so long,* David had cried, sitting on the arm of the couch. This was during one of his returns. After the first exit, he kept going and coming back, spending money at a furious pace. Their money? Each time, she thought, now we'll resolve it. He'd stay at the house and they'd live a sort of together life, eating spaghetti and arguing into the night and sometimes having sex. But then he'd be buying a plane ticket online again. "I've got to clear my head one more time," he said, the second time, when she walked into the so-called study where he'd slept and saw on his face that something was up.

"Have you got someone in Oslo?" she'd asked, her morning voice cracking, mouth dry, thinking that a smarter person would've asked this months ago.

"Gosh, no," he said. This turned out to be true. Or at least no one materialized—maybe no one lasted. And so it repeated, two—three?—more times?

But that is an unpleasant place to dwell, and with a quick leap she is back, instead, in the ancient past—not ancient to her at all, in fact, "ancient" being just a way of talking, of convincing yourself that something was a long time ago even though it, this so-called past, is still moist on your skin.

But there too, of course, there is guilt, like a bad hangover when you're supposed to be sharp at work — pain that you caused yourself and you can't expect any sympathy for. She had tried to purge the reminders of her young life: the train tickets she'd kept from her first trips alone with friends, dumb presents from dumb boyfriends, even the scribbled notes full of inside jokes she had exchanged over the years with her best friend Danijela. She missed those notes later, after she lost her.

Danijela moved to Munich during the war, which was fine, what people did, but then something went wrong. Something unclear. There was a fire in her apartment, and she jumped out. She was in the hospital with broken legs and broken hips. Mira took the overnight bus to Munich. When she finally found the hospital and the right section of the right ward, and then asked the nurse, who was hastily stacking hospital gowns onto a shelf on wheels, about Danijela, the nurse said, gently, Sie ist nur sehr traurig. She is just very sad. This was shocking, partly because Mira had no idea her escape from the fire had anything to do with feelings, and partly because she expected something like, We're monitoring her condition, or even a scolding, like, Don't bring in outside food, because Mira was carrying a small basket of oranges, which she'd picked up at a supermarket she spotted when she got off at the bus stop.

There was a uniformed guard standing by the door of the room with his arms crossed. Danijela was awake; her dark hair fanned around her head, as if she'd spread it out for some edgy or strange photo shoot. Her feet were held in a gummy contraption raised above the bed. Mira put her hand on the sturdy, smooth knuckles of Danijela's left hand.

Looking somewhere below Mira's chin, Danijela said, "I tried to tell people, that it wouldn't —" but she didn't finish that sentence.

"Everybody here is so kind," she said instead.

"Oh, that's good, that's good," Mira said, and stroked her hand.

They were silent until Danijela spoke again. "How is it possible," she said, "that billions of creatures are born on this earth, and have no control over their fate? They fight to survive, and suffer anyway, in the most random, cruel ways, and then die. How can this mean anything?"

Mira said nothing. When a person asks such an astute, yet incomplete question, is there even anything you can say?

She stayed in Munich two more days, in a very dirty hostel, but nothing changed when she visited again. Remember the green sea at Hvar, she said, and the shrimp pesto pasta the Sicilians made us? We'd never heard of pesto nor eaten shrimp before. Remember, remember.

Those are fond memories, Danijela said, but they're like pretty postcards; nothing of that is real life.

The whole bus ride home from Munich, Mira could not get warm. She draped spare shirts and pants over her knees but she shook and shook, until she got off the bus, walked the long walk home — she was staying with her parents again, in the house they were slowly patching up — and immediately got into a very hot bath. Once the warmth moved through her, she wept.

She told her parents all about it afterwards, in a rare outpouring — they'd seen Danijela grow up alongside Mira, and they were the only ones around to talk to.

Mira's mother said, "I never thought she would be one to crack like that. She always seemed sensible — a person you could trust."

The tone, the pursed lip, were familiar. But this time Mira could not bear the cuttingness. So she walked out of her parents' kitchen without a word, still damp under her clothes from the bath. She sat in the park thinking of Danijela's words: How can this mean anything? How can it, how can it?

And that was really how she decided to leave the country. Ljilja had already left, first to Slovenia, then Germany, then Canada, and Mira thought, It's a good time to follow her and get the heck out of this place that everyone has left already anyway.

Until then she had done as most others. When the first grenades fell on her town, she was at home for the summer after a second year away at university. She spent nights in the cellar with her parents, but come fall she found a friend going back to Zagreb and five of them, all young, all women, squeezed into the friend's clunky Renault and drove a tense, circuitous route to get there. More than the occasionally unbearable physical tension she felt in the cellar, she remembers this drive as the hardest of her life. She didn't fully trust that her friend knew the safe routes. They were stopped at checkpoints three times and each time, approaching, knowing there is nowhere to go but through it, no offramp, no second path, Mira thought, She's driven us into occupied territory. They'll pull us out of the car and rape us.

When they made it within Zagreb city limits, the whole carload of them was suddenly alive with laughter. They rolled down the windows and stuck their arms out as if they were headed on a carefree road trip.

But the place Mira had shared with roommates just a few months before now housed two families. She moved five times over that fall and winter. But modified classes continued at the university, and she tried to study and pass her exams.

Her parents wouldn't budge from home. Sometimes she could get a hold of them and sometimes she couldn't, and she began to resent them for the nights she couldn't sleep and the days she couldn't eat or study and the smoking that made her sick. When the back of the house was hit during one early morning strike, taking out most of a bedroom and a good chunk of the roof, it was the worst thing but also the best thing: they had spent the night in the neighbour's cellar and were safe, and then they finally left. They packed what could fit into the car and moved in with Dad's niece a couple of hours west. In another year — during which they moved several times too, because of course the hospitality didn't last — they went home. The war wasn't over, but it had shifted just enough for people to start returning. And so they fixed the roof and sealed off the part of the house that was destroyed and started, very slowly, to rebuild.

But Mira could not imagine living there. Neighbours had disappeared, the street names had changed. The house of her childhood proved impermanent, and unlike her parents, she could not resurrect it for herself. She was six exams short of a degree in South Slavic literatures but those six suddenly seemed like years of work on a fish-gutting factory line. So she got herself to the embassy in Zagreb and filled out the many tedious forms. Most everyone she knew had gone — Mirko was on and off the front for nearly two years, and not in touch, Danijela in Munich, other friends all over the place.

Danijela did make it out of the hospital, into a seemingly quiet life about which Mira now knows little. She heard from her months after they saw each other at the hospital, and since then, they exchanged a phone call or messages every couple of years. The last time they talked was after Mira's dad's funeral.

And that brought her to the present. Dad dead too soon and without forewarning. Mom not entirely well, and far away, and a constant source of worry.

And, at least, since she's not had children, no one will ever have to worry about her in this way when she grows old. But this is less a consolation than another thing to brood about.

Maybe Bernard would worry about her, if she were living alone, far away, and he heard she just collapsed onto the floor one day, with no one there to help her get back up? But Bernard will have his own parents to pick up off the floor, won't he?

"Should we have children?" David had said, unexpectedly, some years into their marriage, while cramming scrambled eggs on toast into his mouth.

"Yes!" It didn't surprise her that she yelled out yes. She'd always assumed they would, at some point.

"When? Like now?" he said.

"I mean, I don't know about right now." Right now was a bit too soon.

He cocked his head, mouth full.

It's not that she had some great other plans or a desire for something people called a career. But she wanted to be ready. Or maybe just footloose a little longer?

He finished chewing and said, "We got time. I should finish my record stand project first."

And they closed the topic satisfactorily, for the time being, happy to have agreed, which, it occurred to her later, was the way they often left things. Should we repaint the living room yellow? Yes, let's! Perfect. Great. And the living room stayed beige for another year, but it never seemed a problem.

If they had had those imagined children, they would — the children — she supposed — structure her life, be the loadbearing wall, the immovable object at the centre of her world. Instead, here she was: a lone tree, stretching her branches into empty air, an unknown beyond. No, that was too dramatic. And she can't decide in this alternate future if she and David and the kids are together, some cheerful and inefficient grouping, or she and a child are eating a plain dinner at a small table, until David texts he's on his way because it's his turn to take them for the weekend.

But, really, she can't picture any of it, because it's such an extraordinary otherworldly dimension, this being a mother — she, her, being a mother! — that she can only picture falling through a door in the floor, whoosh! Ouch! and then. Somewhere other, dark, warm, soft?

It's because you think like this you couldn't manage to have actual children, a voice tells her. Now whose voice is that?

Enough, enough brooding. She gets up off the armchair and brushes her teeth in the funny sink in the corner. She smooths her hair down, pushes her eyebrows up. She should do something, but she's tired. So she finds her tablet, for a little comfort and distraction. I'll just get into bed with it for a tiny bit, she tells herself, reclining against the pillow. I'm jet-lagged, after all.

Through the wall behind the headboard, she hears a cry, brief and high-pitched. Then muffled talking, French. A sob — or maybe a laugh? A child's laugh or a child's cry? Then shuffling, a drawer being shut. The hotel is full of noises, scrapings and creaks and distant voices and, if you pass a room at just the right moment, the whoosh of new sheets being laid down. It's a loose operation: everyone does more than one job, signs in arrivals between delivering cheese triangles and fruit compote at breakfast. Any room change, requests for extra towels or complaints about noise get arranged with a few quick, loud words that bounce between the kitchen, the improvised front desk a few metres away, and a boy on a ladder, fumbling with the curtain rod. The owner is harried and distracted, and that boy fixing the rod, definitely, regularly, high.

Nonetheless — breakfast is served, beds made, guests welcomed and discharged.

She pulls the duvet up to her armpits, turns on her tablet, finds a blog she follows with photos of Canadian wilderness. Soothing, usually, but now distant and flat.

She could call that H&M guy. Possibly he would materialize here within the hour, even. Who cares about his irritating overconfidence, his racism, his lack of self-awareness? When you got people really, really close, did they not shape-shift anyway? Out of their context and your own, in the proximity and insulation created by a bed, sheets, a room in an indifferent city, could you not, then, have a fairly good time?

You could, yes, she knew that. In theory you could. But she couldn't now. For one thing, she's out of the habit, discouraged by the possibility of his form in the doorway looking strange and repulsive. For another, to experience the transformation of proximity, you had to be open. After the separation, she had a brief period of such wild, raw openness. You're like a house with no walls, a man had said to her, on their third date, in a loud pub with television screens mounted from the ceiling, broadcasting a golf tournament. It was maybe the smartest thing he'd said to her, but it wasn't a compliment, and he left before finishing his beer, paying his half of the tab. To be left sitting with half-eaten jalapeno cheese sticks, by a man who was neither very original in his thinking nor a smart dresser, but who you thought should be given a chance, shuts one down indeed. This was dating in your forties, she thought on the way home. Also, she thought, I never want to go inside a pub with televisions again for the rest of my life.

When she connects to Facebook, the first posting she sees is a kitten curled like a snail into a tiny flowerpot. Below, BBC reports the recent deaths of nearly a hundred migrants in the Mediterranean, trying to cross from Africa to Italy.

She imagines holding a baby, baby Bernard, say, and depending on the absolute indifference of the ocean, to reach land.

Next, a video of a Northern Alberta lake after an oil spill. Then a speeded-up video of a complicated appetizer, cheese wrapped in salami wrapped in dough wrapped in more cheese and more salami. Also, a filmed speech by a very young Saudi Arabian émigré who has escaped to Sweden with her parents and fights for girls' rights to schooling. Closer to home, rising water levels of the river Sava in northeastern Bosnia. Then a quote by Rumi about welcoming all experience, pain or pleasure, as a gift; she doesn't know who Rumi is, exactly, but this seems almost worth jotting down. Only she's not quite up to throwing off the covers and looking through her purse for a pen.

Then a video with the caption, Let's circulate and find this scum!! Reposted through three different sources. Did her friend really wish to share this, or is it one of those automatically generated things?

She should know better than to click. A child, maybe one year old, maybe a year and half, sits on a bed, a low frameless bed against a wall, with colourful though faded cushions and blankets; the video is shot from up-close so that you see the bed, the wall, and only half a door in the corner of the frame. The woman sitting on the edge of the bed is in profile, a young woman, slim, in a plain skirt and sleeveless shirt, simple rural clothes, bare arms and legs.

She is hitting the child again and again with the flat of her hand, across their head, their back, their legs. The child recoils and wails. The woman pauses, then hits again.

The mundane reality of the room makes Mira unable to stop watching: a hurriedly made bed; crocheted, pale blue cushion covers; a pilling yellow blanket; strands of hair escaping the woman's practical ponytail.

The woman is relentless: she now uses the cushion to hit the child; the child crawls to the corner, tries to rise to its knees as if it would climb the wall, but is again brought down by a blow, and then curls up, crying and retreating into the corner as if to disappear into it.

Another woman comes in and stands by the door frame, wearing a similar skirt, holding a dishcloth in one hand. There is no sound to the video, but you can see her saying something and the young woman speaking back. It must be warm and bright where they are: everyone is bare-armed and the room naturally lit.

Mira is about to stop the clip, when the child starts to crawl from the corner toward the woman, toward her knees, as if it would climb into her lap.

It's hard to believe. The child puts its chubby hand on the woman's knee and looks up at her.

The woman readjusts, tucks in one ankle under the other leg's knee, and starts hitting again.

Who stood filming with an iPhone for nearly a minute as this went on? What series of human actions brought it to Mira's electronic box?

She is in Paris, for the first and maybe only time in her life. She could be in the Louvre, the Musée d'Orsay, the Luxembourg Gardens. Any garden, for Christ's sake, any street.

But she wishes to weep. The baby moving toward the woman, revising the story, trying again for what it knows it needs, a safe enfolding.

Out, she tells herself, into the streets, don't give in to jet lag, to inertia, to brooding, to impotent, internet-induced rage.

She presses the power button on the tablet, then puts on her shoes.

BERNARD LEANS AGAINST the rough wall of the hotel, runs his thumb over the filter of the cigarette before bringing it up to his mouth. *I miss you in Paris*, he writes in a text. Doesn't send it. He's tired of himself, of the same nervy feeling he's never tried to explain to anyone but Aisha. And recently his counselor. Aisha has always listened, always helped him, and now, he was still a coward, still held back from telling Mira the whole story.

He should have kept the pigeon in his room. The day he'd found that other pigeon, last summer, he'd stood on the tiny balcony of his and Aisha's apartment to admire the pink sky — sunset, his favourite time to go for a run. He would cross the river for the best view, to see the valley and the city stretching beyond both sides of the bridge. He went out the back door, and in the parking lot by the alley, a pigeon tried to fly up and away from him, but then seemed stuck, beating its wings furiously at waist height. Bernard watched as the pigeon landed, its chest rising and falling. Then it tried to fly again. It got higher this time, and beat its wings for longer, but still, noth-ing. Poor guy, he thought, and wondered for a minute, should he do something?

But he'd miss the sunset. And really, the pigeon would do its pigeon thing, the thing pigeons do when hurt, which must involve some process of bird biology and organization way beyond his knowledge, and if he'd not happened to come out the back door right then, well, the pigeon would have been just as well off, no? As he went about his human life, endless pigeons went about their pigeon lives, eating and frolicking and mating and defecating and injuring their wings, and, like, what did he know of any of that?

Then he thought, if it stays put there and can't fly away, maybe it'll get run over by someone pulling out or pulling in to park.

And yet, smart pigeon, it had landed next to the curb between parking spots, where it wouldn't be in the way.

So off he jogged into the sunset, had a great run, appreci-ated the mad beauty of the sky and all the pinks and oranges glowing in the trembling water. When he returned, just as the pinkness was being replaced by the muted blue of dusk, he noticed a great many feathers littering the lot. Strange, he thought, did that little guy try so hard to fly he lost some of his feathers? Then he saw the bird next to the curb: white chicken skin where the feathers had been plucked off, blood and worm-like entrails spilling out, and the black eyes, as blank as they'd looked when it landed for the last time and given up.

He's gone over it enough times in his head. The bird's ugly guts, and his banal failure, like a dumb prelude to the main event.

A woman exits the hotel, a tall woman in tight jeans and a cropped leather jacket. She reaches a hand deep into her purse and comes up with a pack of cigarettes, then lights one quickly. It's the maid, the one who smiled ever so faintly at him in that vacant room earlier.

OUTSIDE THE HOTEL entrance, Mira is taken aback by seeing Bernard, on the sidewalk, smoking a cigarette and laughing along with one of the maids — the one they saw earlier inside a room, wiping a cupboard, who is now wearing a cropped leather jacket and jeans, ready to go home.

They both have their sleeves rolled-up above the elbow, showing beautiful long forearms — all the appearance of lanky, light-hearted creatures.

Bernard was really a very sweet, gentle child.

Maybe someone filmed that woman through a window, without her knowing it, collecting evidence for a custody case.

Yet the camera seemed so close. Mira doesn't know what language they were speaking. The woman who spoke must have said something like, That's enough. Let him be.

Then again, maybe she said, Pick up a watermelon at the market later.

She chooses the Musée d'Orsay because it's open late, and it houses a painting David had wished to see: Léon Lhermitte's *Paying the Harvesters*. A small print of it, which he'd cut out of his art history textbook in university, before they'd met, was magneted to their fridge; a larger poster reproduction hung framed in the hallway. Why it appealed to him, she couldn't say exactly — but where was the need, back then, for analyzing what David liked? The love of this image was as familiar a part of David as his hair or hands, just the thing it was, not needing attention.

Now his preferences return to her painfully solid and textured. She can hardly bear to look at tiny espresso cups and saucers, because they used to give him such pleasure! But the unreasonably large collection they had at home he left behind, like so many other things, when he went to Norway the final time, and she was the one to make a well-padded package and deliver it to a thrift store.

Following the metro map, she makes it a half hour before closing time. She looks carefully through the museum's guide to find the painting, its floor and room, and moves quickly, runs, in fact, up the stairs and down the hallways, thinking how strange to run past all those Cézannes as if she were running past bus stop ads for Gap.

The result is standing in front of *The Harvesters* in its original, non-reproduction glory: the painting is huge, taller than her full height, and wider than it is tall. The six figures are in a courtyard, among farm buildings painted brown and beige. In the right-hand corner, sheaves of wheat laid on the ground. On the left, in the foreground, a man sitting on a rough bench holding a sickle, its large blade pointing up. Seated next to him to the right, a woman, the only woman in the frame. She is seated sideways, her head turned away, at waist level with a man standing right behind her — behind the bench — and handing out coins. She is watching a coin about to leave his thumb and forefinger.

The blue of the woman's apron matches the blue of two of the men's shirts, a denim blue, deliberately inserted into the palette of warm browns and yellows and whites. Only the men wearing blue seem to be in charge of the payment, and for a moment, Mira wonders — who are the harvesters, and who the landowners in this composition?

For the first time, she notices something, and can't believe she's never seen it before. There is a baby in the woman's lap. Only its head is visible, cradled by the woman's palm, thus blending into the beige background of the yard and men's pants.

Of course. How stupid, how almost predictable, to see it now.

Out of nowhere, but not for the first time, she hears her dad's voice: *I don't get it. What's it about?* He would say it of just about any painting or drawing or sculpture. Forget installation art. He only admired the skill of rendering reality with brushes and paint; he admired mastery of any sort, but not the subjective effect.

I don't get it either, she says to him now, I just like the back of the woman's neck.

Tzzt, he might say with his tongue, unaware of doing it.

She hadn't expected it here, but it happens, hearing him speak or anticipating his response to something. In traffic, for instance, when someone changes lanes sloppily. Or at a sidewalk hot dog stand: *That man is a master of hot dogs*, he says to her. Sometimes she is sure he is speaking to her in real space-time; they can get a real back and forth going.

In this way he is like David, hovering about her, there but not there. A woman's voice announces a closing time warning, and Mira steps closer and looks at the woman in the painting once more. It's hard to tell if she's nursing that baby or just cradling it. How often has Mira put on her coat next to that print? Well, it was a pretty dark hallway where it hung. One's eye didn't travel to that wall easily. But why had they not put it elsewhere?

She's sorry to leave, but she has to go to the bathroom. And when she leaves the bathroom, it will be David she will see, leaning against the railing, waiting for her, as he has waited hundreds of times. There he is: he's wearing those skinny black jeans he replaced with the same pair when they wore out, year after year. He raises his eyebrows, as if to say, What next?

I don't know, she answers. It's not fair I have to figure it out all on my own!

I had offered you a plan, hadn't I? Why didn't you take it?

I didn't like it.

Well, it's what I had.

I saw *The Harvesters* up there.

Yeah, I know. I'm here too, can't you see?

It's impressive up close. So big!

Haha. Well, it was just something I liked a long time ago.

A woman's voice announces closing time yet again, David dissolves, and Mira has just enough time to descend the stairs and stand briefly in the huge entryway under the tall dome of the former railway station, facing the preserved Roman numeral clock set high into the grid-work.

David had wanted so much to move to Oslo, and he had presented a mostly feasible plan. His mother was from Russia's Far East, but his father's parents from Norway, so that his dad held Norwegian citizenship and David said he could get it too. This she had doubted. She had a vague sense that the Scandinavian countries were stingy with their citizenship, maybe even with residence and work visas, and what would they care for some offspring born in Canada claiming Norwegian genetics?

"Really," she said, "really?"

The groan he produced was a groan of animal irritation. And it came with a very human eye roll. "Trust me. Jesus."

She still, now, didn't believe it about the citizenship. She also didn't know why to this day she hasn't googled it to find out, or done some basic government website reading.

But, in any case, she could not do it. She couldn't fly over an ocean to land again among strangers with only a fraction of a language — not even that much, this time — in her mouth.

"Imagine," David said, turning back into a friendly animal after his groan. "Just try to imagine. We could get to the Adriatic in three hours. We could go on vacation there three times a year."

More, he said, *the sea*, as any Croatian said of the Adriatic. He understood enough Croatian to understand the threads of conversation.

She said, "Imagine also needing medical care. Going into labour in a foreign country. I don't want to labour in Norwegian!" They were still trying for kids then.

"Are you insane? *Norway*. Not Uzbekistan, or Albania. Norway."

"And my sister, Bernard? What, would I just see them at Christmas?"

"They could visit us. And you'd be closer to your parents."

"I want to see Bernard grow up!"

The animal groan came back. He put his head in his hands, a rare dramatic gesture that appeared during the worst fights.

From behind his hands, he said, "We'll have our own children!"

"It hasn't happened so far." Several times she had dreamt the same dream, small children drowning in shallow puddles.

"No faith," he said, simply and mysteriously.

But she was right that it hadn't happened so far and that they'd even got a referral for a fertility clinic in a city two hours away, and after ultrasounds and samples sent for tests, they were told only that there is such a thing as unexplained infertility.

He'd never before been condescending, much less insulting, as he was during that conversation, and she, shocked, said nothing. The mystery was still how he left it all behind.

The mystery was also how she was as oblivious as she was, like a dumb garden slug, munching away, self-absorbed. He was close to exiting, by then, yet she remained ignorant of the threat, like those children playing in the shallow puddles, in no apparent danger.

By the time she exits the metro, streetlamps have come on. In front of the hotel entrance, Bernard and the girl are still talking. She checks the time on her cell phone: hour and a half, at least. Their postures have shifted, slightly but definitely, so the configuration they make together means something else now. She thinks: they are so young. She could not stand on the street for an hour and a half just to talk to someone, someone she would not even see again. She could no longer believe so effortlessly that a conversation could change her life.

NEXT TO THE MATTRESS on the floor is a low bookshelf doubling as a bedside table, the boards stapled together by hand, the books crammed between them every which way. No other furniture in the room but lamps, four, five, and when Mahue went around turning them on, each corner came to life until there was a glowing whole. It's a tiny room with white bedding and white curtains and a grey-white throw rug, everything soft and textured like crushed cotton; but the walls and floor, except for the rug and that shelf, bare. They sit on the bed like two teenagers, she cross-legged at the head of it, he slouching sideways, both leaning their backs on the wall. She picks up her cup from where it sits on that wobbly bedside shelf but doesn't drink from it, only moves the tea bag string round and round the rim.

He's telling her the story of his Chinese grandparents, who ran a dry goods stand in Saigon, until about 1979, when the authorities seized the rice bags stacked ceiling-high in their house and put them under house arrest. They found a way to sneak out and paid for their place on a smuggler's ship with gold pieces Bernard's grandpa had kept embedded in the wood of a bedroom drawer.

These were details he knew, ones he'd heard from his dad again and again, because he'd asked for them.

But what he's embarrassed about and hopes Mahue won't notice is that — he's just realizing this! — he doesn't quite know why they were placed under house arrest and what politics made them undesirable or vulnerable.

He does know the ship was stormed by pirates, who sent all the men below deck while they ransacked everything.

"When the pirates finished, they let the men come up from below deck and rejoin the women and children, and then the gang added their flag to the ship's mast. That was the custom: then other pirate gangs would know they'd been through and there was nothing left to loot. Imagine!"

"So the men were locked up below, and the women and children on the top deck with the thugs?"

"I think some of the older boys went with the men. My uncle did — I'm not sure about my dad. I think he went with them too."

"Did your grandma ever talk about that?"

"Being separated from them?"

She looks at him with her face unchanged, yet, he thinks, evaluating something. It is a matter of awkward seconds before — like one who gets a surprise tap on the shoulder, and can't imagine who it could be, and then, right, of course, it's obviously so-and-so — he realizes her meaning. He's shocked, and blushes.

"No." He is shocked because it seems extraordinary that such a thing hasn't even occurred to him until this very moment. And also that no one in the family has ever even implied it.

Mahue herself had not come on a smuggler's ship, he learned earlier tonight, but by plane, with a job contract from the hotel's owner.

"It was lucky," she said.

She bends over the edge of the bed to look for something under it, and when she straightens again, she's holding a thin, creased atlas.

"Where did your boat people land?" She turns pages briskly until she is on Asia; he can see she has used this atlas many times before.

"They were on the sea for weeks. They would approach the shore and be sent back. A big ship would pass their little one and they'd think they'd get rescued, but nada. This happened again and again, until, eventually, I guess Malaysia let them dock."

Mahue runs her finger to the coast of Malaysia, moves it back and forth along the coastline.

"On shore, then, the kids went running around looking for clams and shellfish to eat. My dad remembers running back with those clams to his parents, and seeing, in the moonlight, the still bodies of all the adults fanned out on the beach, curled up or lying flat on their backs, like a tableau. Some had fallen asleep, but others had their eyes open and stared, immobile. He said it was the most frightening moment of the whole trip:

all of them still and silent, looking both dead and awake. But I guess someone roused eventually, noticed the kids' hands full of shellfish. And that same night, the men sunk the boat."

How did he have all these details but not the full arc of the story?

"How long did they stay there?"

"The Red Cross arrived. A fence went up and a few outdoor toilets. People filled out forms about where they were willing to go. And then they waited to have their names appear on a list. My dad's family was sponsored by a Baptist church in a small town in Saskatchewan."

She flips to North America, stares at the map of Canada. Their fingers land on Saskatchewan at the same time.

"I like that name," she says. "Anyway, that was a long time ago. But what happens now is the same. Worse."

"Do you know people who came here on smugglers' ships? What about the other hotel workers?"

She takes his hand at the wrist and with her finger traces the vein from the crook of his arm to the base of his palm.

"Look at that," she says, "almost a straight line." It's the first she's touched him, really, and the warm firmness of her fingers circling his wrist is a jolt, the creak of a window opening in a silent room. When he recovers, he points to a small constellation of birthmarks, on the inside of her bicep, which he noticed as soon as she took off her leather jacket when they got to her room.

"But what about this? It's a bit like —"

"No," she says, "don't even try. There is not a constellation you could name that I have not heard these compared to."

The light bulb in the room is dim and he sees Mahue with a slightly fuzzy outline, close enough to him that she is not the person he saw just this afternoon on the stair landing, or even the person he talked to earlier in the evening as the street got darker around them.

"Orion," he says anyway. "Pisces? Ursa Minor. Telescopium."

When she laughs, she flutters her eyes.

"Hopeless," she says, letting the atlas slide to the floor.

ON THE SECOND DAY in Paris, a fine, sunny day, Mira is at the Luxembourg Gardens, alone. Bernard did come down for breakfast, but he was a bear: he joined her table just as she was finishing up and sat there quiet and red-eyed, very slowly torturing a cheese triangle over one half of a baguette.

The only other people in the dining room were an American family of two parents and two either teenagers or young twenty-somethings. They were tall, hefty people, and the kids, a boy and girl, wore that peculiar North American college campus outfit: hoodies and pajama pants and flip-flops. When the girl reached across the table for her dad's Nutella packet, Mira could see her butt crack: no underwear, either. Baffling. Mira saw the girl sneak a look at Bernard as he chewed his baguette, oblivious. Not unusual: girls, women, looked at him all the time. He was tall, and had, as her mother always said, *such a beautiful head.* And he was kind of soft: quick to smile, and possibly, it seemed, eager to please.

The mother of the American family wore a grey head-scarf wrapped turban-like on her head; her face had the shiny, rounded look of someone without hair. The father was wearing a Derreck's Auto Parts ball cap and a striped button-down shirt, and also a permanent nod-smile: a man constantly approving of everything. Seeing Mira looking in their direction, he smiled harder; Mira smiled back; then Bernard looked up and smiled too; finally the mom, the girl, and even the boy caught on to the smile wave, and there: everyone was smiling at everyone, a cross hatch of demented goodwill impossible to get out of.

They were saved, thank God, by a woman who came by to clear the Americans' trays, where crusts and half-eaten jam packets were covered up with the thin paper napkins. That allowed them to transfer their smiles to the server. Even Mira couldn't quite straighten her face as she turned back to her breakfast and made a neat pile of the foil wrappings that had held her cheese triangles.

Only the server was unfazed. This was a woman with smooth, carefully styled white hair and black eyebrows: a striking woman. Yet, familiar-looking. Mira watched her go back to the kitchen.

Bernard went for a sip of his coffee, but then put down the cup in apparent disgust — the milk had formed a film on top. He pulled the film away with a spoon and attempted to wipe it on a napkin. Then he just pushed the cup away from himself, collected his napkin and knife and spoon on the plate, collected the table crumbs too, and set aside the unused jam and Nutella.

Mira saw the American girl sneak another look at him. The girl had blond hair, fair skin, and a small-featured, pretty, unmemorable face. Mira thought: a bland, common Anglo-Saxon face. And also, immediately: who thinks like that? She would never say such a thing out loud.

What she was actually curious about was the woman Bernard was talking to last night in front of the hotel, but that was just another thing that was none of her business.

She didn't want to leave him alone. She asked what he would like to do. When he nixed the Eiffel Tower, she suggested a search for famous graves at Pere Lachaise.

"Edith Piaf rests her soul there," he said.

Rests her soul there. Really, the wit of young people.

"Right, Edith Piaf! I've seen a movie about her."

"I don't know. I don't know which Paris I'm interested in. No, actually, I'm just tired. I'll try to go back to bed for a little bit. It's okay if you go on without me."

She was disappointed, because, especially after last night, she wanted to have a nice day with him. Or did she want him to confide in her all his heartache and worry and make her feel like her life meant something?

Now, sitting in this garden, alone, it occurs to her she shouldn't have listened to him. That him saying she should go on without him was one of those statements that people say when they actually mean the opposite. But he did look weary, and stuck in someplace she had no access to, and so she let him go to his room and she went to her own, where she searched Google maps for the way to the Tower. She made a pitstop when she discovered on the map that the Luxembourg Gardens are very close to the hotel, so she'd be available if Bernard texted and wanted to do something after all.

Now she sits on a chair in the shade of a palm tree, resting her feet on another chair she's pulled up. She looks out at low groomed hedges, pebbles blanched by the sun, large flower plots filled with petunias, daffodils, baby's ear. She decides Paris is about lines and symmetry. About width, but also perimeters: a sense of openness, and yet careful enclosures, iron fences and flower trims. One lawn is free for sitting but another one has a sign warning people to keep off the grass; when a few naïve or entitled tourists don't, a stern man in a stiff blue uniform is immediately on scene, blasting a whistle blow fit for a military drill. Is there any corner of wilderness here? Only these chairs — iron, painted pale green — are a free for all, strewn about in pairs and singles and circles, facing different directions. People arrange their pleasure — they set a chair to face the fountain, use another as an awkward back rest for sitting on the ground.

She is happy to have discovered this place, because the deliberate design, prim beds of annuals, and perfect grass remind her of a garden she used to take Bernard to when he was just a toddler. It was a garden on the grounds of the provincial museum. She was twenty-four, twenty-five years old, just beginning to understand some unexpected things about her new country.

She'd arrived bewildered and wary. She had abandoned her degree and with it the life she had vaguely imagined: some position at the university? Late night conversations with friends, and a small nice flat in Zagreb full of books? Mirko somewhere in there, a lover, a confidant. Then the war and all its shocking changes took away most of the pieces needed for that vague future. Landing in Canada, she felt like her life had fast-forwarded and she'd been cheated of its content.

But then something shifted. When Bernard was born, she fell in love with him, and none of the other stuff, neither the strangeness nor the fear, mattered. She couldn't have expected it, and hardly had the words for what was happening; she only went around saying, I'm wild about that baby! The unlikely wonder of him: when everything had been worn out and precarious, he was robust — robustly alive, and safe. Her sister Ljilja was calm, Bernard's dad Dennis quiet and loyal and industrious; both were young but determined, certain of themselves, of Bernard, of their tiny fixer-upper house, of the nest they were padding for him.

And he was such a sweet child. When you fed him Nutella crepes, he made you take a piece to share. When telling you of a game he wanted to play, he'd say, I have a tuydea! He said, tuydea, bezombies, besatisfaction. Her sister said it's a mild articulation delay, but it was also adorable. And he was this kind of kid: he absorbed everyone's gestures and delivered perfect imitations, not even aware of the copying. To be honest, he would say, cocking his head and scrunching his mouth, channeling his mother, I'm not sure that is such a good tuydea.

That, and the gentleness of him: you could give this kid the blindest, tiniest kitten. Mira remembers the earnest concentration with which he lowered his hand to touch a puppy —

an open hand, receiving the animal more than petting it. She trusted him with any jewellery, the fine gold chain from her godmother she cherishes and wears still, which he would run his finger over when he sat in her lap, one, two years old. He would never close his fist and yank. He never yanked on or pushed a thing in his whole little child's life.

And soon after Bernard was born, she suddenly found friends. She reluctantly — because she was still self-conscious about her English — accepted an invitation to go see a band with the hotel kitchen crew, and among them was David, this funny, skinny line cook, figuring out his life post-university. And she was young again. She didn't go to university, but she started to read books again, and she had late night conversations with friends, and she had a lover.

Love and love. Like Bernard, David was all new, and un-damaged. They married quickly, surprising everyone, in a cere-mony they were proud of — no church, no hall, no long white dress! They invited a handful of friends, and Ljilja's family, to a picnic in a clearing by the river where they had spent time in endless talk and making out after they met. The friends brought a cooler of mini bottles of sparkling wine. Bernard, in fire truck shorts and a blue bowtie, had handed them the rings. How transgressive it had seemed at the time, and how not so now. Her parents didn't make the long trip. Did they wish to come? She could not answer for sure.

And David loved Bernard too. What good pretend-parents they made when they took him on the weekends: clapping their hands at the bottom of the slide or intertwining their arms at the movie theatre over Bernard sucking on his juice box in the seat between them.

The memory of Mirko was then only a few years in the past, and she would catch herself in that then-recent, but across-the-ocean past. Because, in a fine quasi-symmetry, Mirko had a little brother (must have him still; he would be older than Bernard by just a handful of years), a red-headed, chubby little boy, a pre-menopausal accident, brought up by two begrudging parents, and she and Mirko also played pretend-parents to him. When someone at home had a headache, Mirko and Mira put the boy on the back of one of their bikes and rode to an ice cream shop in town. They loved it when the woman scooping out their chocolate and vanilla teased them that they'd make good parents; they were nineteen, twenty years old, playing.

And, now in Canada, she'd get caught in the same tableau with David and little Bernard, only this boy was thin and dark-haired. She on one side of the boy with David/Mirko on the other, saying the same things and playing the same games, like there had been no time. Her fingers walking up the boy's arm and hurrying under the chin to tickle, his wild giggles, her endearments in Croatian, bebane, mišu mali. It was dizzying, and exuberant.

She didn't answer Mirko's one letter, an extraordinary letter, that arrived at her sister's address in Canada, though she did read it. It was the longest communication she'd had from him since he'd gone away to the front. Was it too much for her to bear, to know the things he told her? Was she out of her depth and that's why she didn't write back?

With time, the tableaus changed. Before Bernard even started kindergarten, Dennis, who was still loyal and quietly pleasant, suddenly became no longer industrious but mysteriously depressed and unemployed. Ljilja, who had spent the first years of Bernard's life either on extended maternity leave or working only occasionally, now added a full-time job to her occasional accounting work so that they might keep the house.

Until then, Bernard had been always by her side, on her hip or by her feet as she loaded the washer or brushed her teeth. And Mira, at first angry at Dennis, wondered: was some part of Ljilja glad to be forced to get out of the house? Because she'd sensed conflict in her before. Ljilja would ask that Mira and David take Bernard, in a tone that suggested all she needed in life was just one darn afternoon to her own self, but when they did, she could hardly let them get out the door without additional kisses, reassurances, extra juice cups and pants.

But what did Mira know — this was probably just what it is to parent.

"Can Dennis take antidepressants?" Mira asked one afternoon, a year into this situation, as she and Ljilja made little balls of Bernard's socks.

Ljilja stopped, unexpectedly upset. "He is taking antidepressants." She threw a sock ball into the basket. "You think it's so simple."

"All I mean is, it's not fair to you. You can't do everything. Like, how long can this go on?" She paused and then dared. "I mean, if you want to leave him, I —"

Another sock ball flew toward the basket, bounced off the edge.

"Oh great. Great. Then I'll work two jobs and pay for daycare and have what to look forward to? Also, he does make food sometimes, if you haven't noticed. Also, people do recover from depression. You don't drop a husband because they're sick."

Mira felt chastised, but maybe not enough. When next she and David came by, this time only to drop off some herbal concoction she'd got at the farmer's market for Ljilja's sore neck, they found Dennis alone in the living room. Mira looked through the half-open door of the bedroom, and there was Bernard, sitting on his parents' bed, loading up little cars onto a battery-operated truck with a moving ramp.

"Are you staying?"

"Not this time, sweetie, we —"

"Can we go somewhere?"

"Maybe tomorrow!"

He was still staring. She remembers trying to understand — was it pleading in his eyes?

"But maybe we could go today. I've already got a shirt on."

She sat down next to him.

"Look," he said. He drove another car with his hand onto the ramp, then pressed one of three buttons, and the ramp lifted, beep beep beep, and the cars came down.

"That's awesome!"

Why did he not at least play in the living room, where his dad sat, barefoot and unshaven, but in clean clothes, occasionally changing a CD in the stereo?

Mira took to finding excuses to drop in at various times when Ljilja was working, to see how, indeed, Bernard spent his days.

"Hey," Dennis would say each time, "good to see you," as friendly as always, ordinary. Never annoyed. "Bebe is in our room loading up his trucks. You know him." And he'd smile as they were sharing a moment about Bebe's cute peculiarities.

The sun has moved at the Luxembourg Garden, and so she shifts her two chairs to follow the shade. Near her, on a homey woolen blanket spread over pebbles, a teenage couple — couple, not friends, she is sure — is involved in an intense embrace, but non-sexual, an embrace of consolation, the one girl's head pressed hard into the other's collarbone, arms coiled around shoulders and waist, their eyes closed.

After leaving her, on the echoing phone line from overseas, David had said, "I dream I am looking for you, you are very close, someone directs me through another room and there you are, in a corner, but you turn and it isn't you at all."

She remembers how he'd pushed Oslo on her because it's closer to Croatia. If she lived in Paris, she'd also be closer — closer than in Canada, definitely. She could fly with one of those cheap airlines with small planes that don't let you take any luggage with you. Could she live in Paris? Look at this park.

Mirko may well live within walking distance of this park. How much French could she survive on?

Her phone buzzes and when she looks at it she sees an email, but not the one she wants — this one from a work friend, checking in; except that the checking in devolves into a recounting of the newest on a show she watches, *The Real Housewives of Kentucky*. "I know it's dumb," the friend writes, "but at the end of the day that's all my brain can handle."

Mira closes her eyes. When did this happen, that talking about the plot of *The Real Housewives of Kentucky* became acceptable conversation?

"Also," her friend says, "the Zen Beast is on a mission. She's reorganizing the office spaces. I think you and me both might be booted into the back chambers. Not to ruin your vacation."

Mira's new boss was a soft-spoken woman who signed off on emails with "Be well." Yet in barely two months, she'd found three inefficiencies in the form of people, who disappeared with no warning, being made to clear out their desks after hours under watch of a human resources employee. Mira has been with the Registrar's Office for some eleven years. She did not want to be next. But it's always like that, she thinks. Someone is always booting you out of where you just got comfortable.

On the other side of the large fountain, through the glare of sun, she recognizes the well-curved ball cap shield and the protruding stomach of the American dad from the hotel. Even from here she can see he's smiling. He's taking a picture of his wife by the fountain, her greyish headscarf blending into the background of spraying water, her orange tank top glaring against it. He holds the small camera carefully in his large hands, and she stands still, patiently, until he brings the camera down. Then he looks around and approaches a young woman walking by; as she takes the camera from him, he touches his hand to his ball cap shield and nods. At first, he and his wife hold hands as the woman aims the camera at them, but then, suddenly, as if on second thought yet simultaneously, they send their arms all the way around each other, her hands scrunching his shirt to hold on to as much of his girth as she can. Even when the woman has taken several pictures, they don't let go, not until she's standing in front of them, returning their camera.

Mira's phone buzzes again — a continuous buzz, a phone call. But the angle and glare of the sun — she must've lowered the screen brightness? — makes it impossible to see who it is. Air catches in her throat. Would she recognize Mirko's voice?

"Mira, it's you." Her mother speaks very quietly then suddenly very loudly. "I didn't think I would get a hold of you," she yells.

"You shouldn't have phoned — your phone bill will be too high."

"Can you phone me back so it bills you?"

"No, it's a cell, it costs a lot — I mean I don't know how much it costs — I'm in roaming."

"Oh."

"Are you alright?"

"The television has broken down. We've had so much rain here. You don't think the rain can affect the antennae, do you?"

"Oh, what the heck."

"I was watching that show, you know, *Love is on the Farm*, those clowns. You haven't seen it, have you?"

"No. Did —"

"I mean, these women competing for the love of three bachelor farmers. They can't tell a bed of bean stalks from a strawberry patch! But I'd have some words for those men too: who do they think they are? Wanting a woman who knows the land, who looks good, and, like that one tubster, even a woman to play his old piano and arrange bouquets for their dinner table. Really. The only one who could have done that, in my opinion, was voted off last week. But they should get a little less squeamish if they want to earn a husband, you know — they way that one nearly retched when the poor calf was being born — well, that'll get you voted off. It was gross, of course. But why come on the show? Some people, really, are all wrong about themselves —"

"Did you ask that guy — Anica's son — to try fixing it?"

"Well, last time I lost reception, he worked on it, and who knows that he didn't damage something? He was the last one to touch it."

"Well, that was forever ago."

"It's been reliable for almost twenty years, this television. Now, when I can't do my gardening outside, or do much else, it breaks down. Like the stroke wasn't —"

And then she is retelling the story of the stroke — mini-stroke, as the doctor called it, a transient ischemic attack.

Her mother has always worried about the phone bill, so why now the extravagance of calling her, in France, to tell her the same story?

"We'll be there soon enough. Just hold out two more days."

"But are you well — is Bernard well?"

Mira is surprised by this worry.

"We're fine," she says softly.

"Is it raining over there? The rain here just doesn't stop. I don't understand it."

But Paris is as sunny as a postcard.

"No, it's hot here."

"There's rain on the other side of the border in Bosnia too, Anica told me, and Sava has never been this high. They're worried about flooding over there. I can't sit in the yard, you know, the wind even pushes the chairs around — and you can imagine my poor flowers. Your dad and I used to do that, I'd bake in the morning and then we'd go sit outside with some sweets and have our second coffee and —"

"Yes."

"I'm making a Sacher cake for when you arrive. I walked to the corner store, you know, I need to keep up my walking. Maybe when you come, we'll be able to have our cake out there. It can't rain forever, can it?"

"We'll see you so soon."

"Take care of yourselves. All the terrorism these days —"

"Don't worry about the terrorism — or the television. We'll get a new one when we come. They're cheap now."

After they say goodbye, she lets the phone drop into her purse, at her feet. That goddamn half-ton crusher television. After twenty years of doing its job, now of all times — but she realizes she's thinking exactly what her mother just said. She should've asked her if she's got a good stock of magazines, those home decorating ones, or the lifestyle ones she likes so much, with pictures of socialites' seaside vacations. She could phone someone to drop some off, perhaps?

It was good luck that, when the stroke happened, the neighbour, Anica, was over at the house. They were at the door, saying goodbye, when Mom opened her mouth and no words came out. Then she swayed, reached for something to steady her and, finding nothing, fell — slowly, Anica told Mira later, like she was folding herself onto the floor. By the time the ambulance came, Mom was conscious and sitting in a chair. Scared, Anica said, I could tell your mom was scared. They kept her at the hospital for the next two days, anticipating a full-on stroke. Leonarda insisted on a third and fourth day of monitoring.

Mira was grateful for Anica. But the thing about extraordinary luck is how close it brings you to the brink — the *what if* of no one being there. What if, indeed, no one is there next time?

But the truth is, the truth might be, that she doesn't quite, doesn't entirely, consistently, care, not exactly in the way that she should.

The truth is, she seems to be coming up against something inside herself. Though perhaps it has been there all along, this feeling, which is there in the way that the distant roar of traffic and sirens, or the electric buzz of a fridge, or the sound of wind and seagulls is *there*? You just think that this something, this background noise, doesn't need your attention.

But maybe it does, maybe the sirens are coming to your door and the wind portents a storm headed for your street.

The sun is bearing down on Mira's head again. Paris is indeed as sunny as a postcard — not a hint of rain here. The young couple on the blanket shift arms and legs. Suddenly she thinks she was wrong earlier — consolation can be sexual, can't it?

She rises from her chair. The sun could make her doze off, sleep away half an afternoon in Paris, which feels as wasteful as sleeping through a month of time at home. The Americans are walking around the fountain, away from the park, slowly, holding hands, not hustling to get anywhere. Given that she's wearing sunglasses, she finds it hard to imagine they would notice and recognize her, but they do — they turn their heads just enough to notice her standing there and, echoing the morning, they wave and smile.

"Where are your youngsters?" she calls out.

They pause, and she's not sure if they've heard her. Then the dad yells, "Oh, too lazy to go anywhere this morning!"

"Mine too — napping!"

They all shake their heads, smile more, wave more, and the two walk slowly away.

And what indeed is Bernard doing? She sends him a text telling him to get in touch when he's up. It's still morning, after all. Maybe they could go to the Musée d'Orsay together, and she could see *Paying the Harvesters* again. Maybe Bernard would have something smart to say about it? It bothers her that she might've discouraged him from talking last night, and now she was embarrassingly eager to know he wouldn't stay closed to her forever.

She checks her map and starts walking toward a metro station on Boulevard Raspail. She gets on the metro, but then on a whim gets out early, to walk along the Quai d'Orsay, by the Seine. If Bernard gets in touch, she can get back on the subway easily and be back at the hotel in just a short while.

But she almost regrets the walk. For a while it's marvellous to stroll in a place where everything, the bridge railings and window shutters and café chairs and garbage cans, is new, or almost new, but she underestimated the distance. By the time she is nearing the Eiffel Tower, she's parched, her blouse sticking to her back, her feet hurting, the old pain in her ankle surfacing. Why has she made herself suffer so much?

The closer she gets to the grounds, the more crowded it is. There are more and more men walking around with giant key rings; each ring is looped with hundreds of tiny key chains in the shape of the tower. On the small patches of grass beside the sidewalk, other men have spread other such wares, endless miniature reproductions: the tower inside a heart, the tower glittering with little pink faux diamonds, the word Paris with the "a" made to look like the tower. The real tower — or the original one, or just the biggest one? — rises behind them, above the lush foliage of tall trees. Among the keychains for sale, there are also, inexplicably, mechanical toy puppies: one man winds up a brown and white one so that it runs in a circle and barks, looking distraught more than cute. The puppies cost five euros, the keychains, one, two, or three, depending on size. Is it possible anyone makes any money doing this? The tourist crowds get thicker as she gets closer to the entrance, but hardly anyone stops to buy anything; hardly anyone looks at the crazed mechanical pups, or even at the men themselves.

Mercy is spotting a man selling a couple of water and pop bottles alongside his spread of keychains. Seeing her look, he points to the mini-Eiffels; she points to the bottles, and after several finger-points they land on water. He holds up three fingers. But while she's digging in her change purse for coins, a sudden commotion rises, like a bad wind: men turn their heads in agitation and call out to each other. Some are rising to their feet. The man in front of her drops the bottle he was about to hand her and stands up. Then more yelling across the grass, in languages she does not understand. The passersby look on curiously, bemused and deciding whether to get alarmed. Police, someone says in English, and she turns in the direction others are looking: blue and red flashing lights approaching quietly, without sirens.

And then, a magic trick: the blankets the trinkets are on turn out to have handles on the sides, and the men — dozens of them, most of them, including the one right in front of her — grab these handles, instantly gathering a hundred tiny Eiffel

Towers into a single sack that each slings over his shoulder. It happens impossibly fast, the grass bare, the men running. They run diagonally across the road, then up the opposite sidewalk, some turning a corner and others sprinting straight ahead. Each man to himself. Two police cars follow in the same two directions the men have split into. She can see the soles of the men's flip-flops flashing as they run.

The rest of the people also look on. The bad wind blows only for some.

She stares in their direction for a long time. Eventually she picks up the water bottle that fell on the grass and that she didn't pay for and guiltily sits down with it on a shaded bench, then looks on the map for the nearest metro back to the hotel. She turns her head to look at the Eiffel Tower rising above the trees, but doesn't reach for her phone — what was the use in taking a photo?

Just as she's figured out the metro, a tall Black man stops near her, with, yes, impossibly, a jangle of mini-Eiffels strung on a large ring, which he holds up to her with one hand. Mira, confused by his presence, tilts her head in an apologetic no.

The man says, "Ti, Zagreb?"

"What? Sort of."

"Dobar den. I studied in Zagreb. Student exchange. Before your war."

"You look too young!"

He smiles widely, as if knowing it. "Zagreb nice," he says, and walks off, the rustle of the keychains receding along with him.

AFTER A LONG MORNING spent almost entirely in bed, occasionally texting with Mahue, regretting texting Mahue, then
also writing and erasing texts to Aisha, Bernard finally feels
better. He's lost time, yes, that's not great, but he's got two
more days, and he's mapped them out. In the evening he'll take
Mira to the crazy pizzeria on Rue de Buci, where he and Aisha
ate on their second day in Paris. The afternoon, he's spending
in Montmartre.

When he and Aisha rode their bikes into Montmartre, last
summer, to see the Sacré-Coeur, they found things were less
manicured. More immigrants — they overheard, everywhere,
languages they didn't recognize. After the church, after the
relentless streams of people flowing in both directions, the
buskers with guitars and others with great collections of shiny
rosaries, they'd found an overgrown, weedy place behind what
they took to be a church office. They unlatched an old gate
and went in.

It was silent in there, and the trees were so large and full that it was dusky, nearly dark — a cool, verdant darkness. They dropped their bikes and lay on the moist ground.

Now, how could he find that place again?

He's cheating a little, having taken the metro. As he walks the street leading uphill toward the church, the Sacré-Coeur looks just as he remembers it: a sugar hill surrounded by ants. He's one of many trudging toward it. He's also sort of on the lookout for a stationery shop, or someplace he might get a postcard, but around here it's all fabric shops and tiny meat markets and beauty salons. He should have remembered that. The shops are dusty and give off a smell of stale plastic and cheap fabric — what was that smell? Some kind of chemical? Isn't that something he should know?

Aisha had texted him in the morning while his head was in the crook of Mahue's elbow. Mahue was not asleep, or not soundly, anyway: she'd open her eyes, turn over, stare for a while, close her eyes, and so on again and again. Each time she'd pull along some part of him and thus they stayed intertwined. Eventually she swung her legs over the edge and padded to the bathroom. He told himself he wouldn't, but he did, he reached out for his phone, under the nest of his clothes.

The text said, *I can't believe it about the wine stain. Too much. Maybe you need to steal that duvet, like everyone steals towels. I hope it's not too hard for you, being there. Miss you.*

It would have been about eight in the evening back home, eight hours earlier than Paris, and Aisha would have been — what, doing what? He didn't know about the shape of her days any more. He still phoned her sometimes, but not late at night when she was likely to be in bed, and not alone. When she wrote to him, she always said, *I, me*, never *we*, never including the veterinarian.

And Bernard never mentioned him, nor gave him the definitiveness of a name. Why should he? It's enough that he saw the bastard's ass when — well, when will he ever erase that from his mind?

But all that was just the misery of four a.m. — the lizard brain acting up, as Aisha would say.

Mahue had shuffled back, still wearing his t-shirt.

"What's wrong?"

Did women have some weird sixth sense, some preternatural emotional intelligence? He rubbed his four-a.m.-eyes, said, "Nothing at all, I'm very happy, I like your t-shirt."

He hated early mornings, and goodbyes. But it wasn't goodbye yet; there was still time to take a t-shirt off and put one on.

When it really was the morning, with both of them wearing their own clothes, she said, "This is probably stupid to bring up, but at the hotel, you know, don't act like this happened, like you know me."

"Of course not."

"It's just my job, you understand."

"Of course. I'm sorry."

"If I thought you should be sorry, I wouldn't have invited you here."

It was a cold walk back to the hotel. In his room, he typed and erased, typed and erased, and then, filled with an unexpected, diffuse self-loathing, came down to breakfast. Mira was kind, but he couldn't bear the way she was looking at him in that concerned and eager way that was also trying to hide how concerned she was with just what was going on. Which just reminded him how foolish he must seem.

So he took a nap. This used to be his dad's solution for everything—lie down for a bit. Really, it's worked remarkably well for most of Bernard's life.

On the street, the people walking ahead of him have stopped suddenly. Everyone's looking up: a man is running down a street perpendicular to theirs, being chased by two others. In the moment Bernard sees them, the two whip out wrenches from their back pockets without breaking stride. The man ahead of them is running with the intensity of a sprinter, his chest puffed out, legs leaping. On both sides, the passersby freeze, as if stopped at a train intersection. But it's all a moment, a surreal interruption: the train passes and the tourist traffic continues. Untouched, it seems: only a couple of shopkeepers stand looking after the men, hands on hips, shaking their heads.

He's standing next to a tiny supermarket. There, right in front of him, walking from the opposite direction, that girl, the very one with Aisha's nose, walks into the shop. The girl's skirt has a pattern of hearts in boxes at its hemline: a train of box cars with heart shapes. Without thinking why or what he'll do, he follows her inside.

He finds himself immediately in what seems to be the juice aisle. Pop aisle? Shelves of drinks in bottles and Tetra Paks, in many colours and with names he can't read. He walks around it and is then in the snack aisle. People are actually buying things, like this mom and two boys in front of him, and he is in their way, a fake shopper, the chip bags crinkling as he tries to move past them. At the end of the aisle, he's stuck behind someone else, two men with full baskets, and as soon as that backlog clears, he heads back around, past the drinks and outside, feeling rather like a tool. But a moment later, he hears the door behind him, and there she is, the girl. She stands next to him and looks him up and down. Oh no.

"I saw you," she says, in French. He blushes, yes, indeed. She smiles, perhaps with amusement, or is it derision?

God help him with his French. "I'm Bernard. What's your name?"

She looks down the street, then back at him, and angles her head, as if pointing in a direction. When he doesn't respond, she does it again, and turns to begin to walk. She looks at him again, so he makes a step in that direction, uncertain. Then, yes, she's walking, and he is too, behind her, tentatively. She says something he thinks means, "There's a better place to talk nearby." She turns again, to look behind her, beyond him, and then heads left into an alley. He's not sure. But once they're in the alley, a quiet place with plastic bags of garbage next to the floor mats at the back doors, she slows down, and says, "I'm Janina." Pause. "Where are you from?"

"Canada."

Now they're walking side by side.

"Next to America," she says, and continues. "I came from Bulgaria — you know, Bulgaria?"

"Yes, my mom is from Croatia. How long have you lived in Paris?"

"Oh, years now."

He's relieved that he must've spoken well enough for her to understand him. Then they're out of the alley, and on the street, she silences, looks ahead of her. They walk like that for a bit, him disturbed by her apparent tenseness, not sure how much farther he should go, but not yet ready to stop. They turn a corner past a building, and then they're in a clearing, a not very wide stretch of grass between the building and the next street. She stops by a small hollow in the grass — as if a hole had been dug, and then forgotten, and then reclaimed by grass and weeds. Down into the hollow she slides, and he slides after her.

Sitting at the bottom, their heads just high enough to be eye level with the ground, she seems to relax. She sits sideways with her knees bent, leaning on her palm.

"Are you staying in a hotel?" she says.

"Yes, in — down by — near the Sorbonne — the Luxembourg Gardens?"

She laughs then, says, "I know English too, a little bit, you can say in English and I will say in French."

"Thanks, okay —"

"What's it like in a hotel?"

"Like —"

"How often do they change the sheets?"

"Sheets, yes — I think usually every day, although this hotel is not, well, you know, fancy."

"Are the sheets perfumed?"

"Sorry —"

"Do the sheets smell good?"

He's surprised at the quick questioning. Surprised at the earnestness of it.

"Do they bring you breakfast in your room? Like under those big bells? With big white napkins?" She mimics a server holding a tray, lifting a lid, and he gets it.

"No! No. They do have breakfast though. You go downstairs to eat it."

He's getting into this now.

"What is it?"

"It's a baguette, cut in half, and you get spreads — I mean butter, jam, cheese. Also peaches in a can."

"You have to put the butter on yourself?"

He doesn't quite get this, but says, "It's in a little packet, like so," and makes a box with his fingers. "And you get coffee, or tea."

"In nice cups?"

He moves his head to say, so-so. "Not bad."

"And you all sit around a big table?"

"Small tables. For two, maybe four people."

"Do you go to school? University?"

"I did. I do."

"What happens there? What do they talk about?"

"Well —"

This is tough. He can't tell exactly how much English she understands and in French he's missing many necessary words. But he doesn't want to lose her.

"Depends on what you study. Say, if you study history, then you listen to a lot of lectures and write essays about them."

"Hm."

"And some classes are big and some are small. You write exams." Why hadn't he given French more attention in his life so they could talk properly? "You go to the bar after classes. Or maybe you have to go to work."

"Work?"

"You probably have a job. Like, in a bar or in a store."

She looks shocked at this. She flicks the dandelion stalk she'd been twisting with her fingers, gone soft from the handling, and yanks out a clover.

"You've never — you've never been to a university?"

She shakes her head.

Up close, in the clarity of daylight, she seems older than he'd imagined her to be, with slight lines around her mouth, and two furrows forming between her eyebrows. She moves a strand of hair from her forehead, pulls it tight behind her ear, then reaches into a pocket — who would think that skirt has pockets? — and comes up with a plastic bag of pumpkin seeds. She folds back the opening of the bag and extends it toward him.

He reaches in, pulls out a few seeds between his fingers. "Sure, that's funny, my mom loves —"

"I work too. Sewing, mending, you know, I'm good at that. Fixing shoes, purses. Cleaning — they always need someone to clean toilets."

She takes a single pumpkin seed and puts it into her mouth, as if sucking the salt, and puts the bag away.

She asks about his jobs, and then where he buys clothes. He realizes he's gone sweaty from the sun and the effort of finding the words.

When she gets quiet for a little while, looking off, he dares to ask, "Was it you, the other day, on the Champs-Élysées, in front of the Chanel store?"

She shrugs. He's sorry he's asked, because it changes her calmly pensive face. "It doesn't matter," she says.

He doesn't know if *it* is being her, or the whole business of doing that, kneeling on a rich and famous street, asking passers-by to put change into a paper coffee cup for you. "Where do you live?"

"Here, there. You have to keep moving. Paris — people like us can't stay too long in one place."

He meant merely to reciprocate and show interest, but her tone, suddenly impatient, makes him think he's been intrusive. He must be right, because she rises suddenly and brushes grass and dirt from her skirt.

He rises too. "Do you have to go? I really enjoyed —"

Clipped around her waist she wears a black pouch, the kind men travellers wear, and now she unzips it and pulls out a cracked-screen phone from it. She swipes, taps, then surprises him by reaching out for his arm.

"Oh!" He laughs as she pulls him near and with an extended arm takes a selfie of their heads. But because of the glare of the sun, he could only see a black-grey emptiness where there faces should've been.

"Selfie!" she says, and laughs too.

"Do you think it worked, should I take one with my —" he starts to pull out his own phone, but she is already climbing up and out.

When he follows, hoping it's not really over, she points him in a direction, mimics a right turn with her arm, waits to make sure he understands, which he acknowledges he does, even though he'd like to say something else. And before he's said anything at all, she is off, walking quickly, almost running.

AFTER THE EIFFEL TOWER, Mira had a dizzy, foggy feeling, perhaps from too much sun. Descending into the shady, humid coolness of the metro station should have been a relief, but wasn't — the stairs stretched with endless, dizzying repetition; footsteps and hollers echoed disjointedly. There were hurriedly approaching, urgent thumps, and slowly receding, persistent heel-clicks; an inchoate holler from unclear direction echoed forever, seeming to come and go. She kept thinking of the tall man — how did he know to pick her out as Croatian? And the flashing soles and lumpy sacks of the men, on their way to disappearing down the street.

She made it back to the room and shut the heavy curtains to block out all the light. Lying on the bed with a cold towel pressed to her forehead, she looked up the roofing company's website again, held the phone high above her head and stared at the picture. The name was right, but was it her Mirko? She had recognized him when she first saw it. But the more she looked at it now the more it seemed that any face could look like any other face. She enlarged the picture, and it distended into fuzzy pixels.

Bernard finally appeared, in the late afternoon. He carried a small plastic mesh basket of strawberries. They were dark red and soft, with the tiniest seeds. They were also a kind of shock: a sudden recollection of what *strawberry* could mean, something immediately delicious and completely pleasing. Not the grotesquely large and hard and watery strawberry simulation she bought in supermarkets throughout the long Canadian winter.

She was relieved to see him and cheered by the berries. But now he's brought her to this two-storey pizzeria, an enormous, loud place, the kind of place she hates. She let Bernard choose it, because he said he had good, cheap pizza here last summer, and she didn't want to spoil things with him by insisting on somewhere else. The waiters are theatrical: they carry pizzas high above their heads, fake-drop them, send them sliding along tables so that customers jump just as the plate stops short of tumbling over the edge. People look spooked when the pizza lands, wary of eating it. No care for the waiters, that — they're moving on already, shouting at each other — or shouting, in any case, without it being clear at whom or why. Mira would like to throttle every one of them, or at least snatch the trays from their wild arms and tell them, as you would a five-year-old, to just settle down.

And at a table right next to theirs, a young woman is FaceTiming, in between bites of tortellini, with her iPhone propped up against the enormous salt and pepper shakers. On the other end is a little girl, so that the brief pauses in the waiters' antics are filled with the girl's high-pitched voice and the young woman's cooing and smitten laughter.

Bernard, at least, seems improved compared to this morning, energetic: his clothes are crisp and he eats with a teenager's appetite, sandwiching the pizza slices and getting them down with quick bites.

Even so, Mira is worried. She's worried about the Aisha thing, and also because it's occurred to her that Bernard is an idealist. On the walk to the restaurant, he told her how he went out to Montmartre, and saw that same girl — does she remember, the one they saw on the Champs-Élysées, in that crazy beggar's pose, who looked like Aisha?

She's from Bulgaria, he said, shocking Mira — shocking her with the revelation that he talked to her. But her family's been in Paris for years, he said. She has to move about — not good to be seen in the same place a lot, apparently. In any case, she also does all kinds of work — fixing shoes and purses, for instance.

He talked to her, he said, for a while, using both English and his elementary school French, and though, at first, she eyed him both suspiciously and curiously, curiosity won.

Even the confidence of starting that conversation dazzles Mira.

"We shared a bag of pumpkin seeds, you know, the kind my mom always eats," he said, just as they were taking their seats on the hard wooden benches of this funhouse.

Mira thinks she understands this much about Bernard: he thinks people are not that different from each other regardless of where or how they'd formed their first words or what they ate or where their faith lay. He believes the rich countries of the world should open their borders, immediately, and all people should settle where they wish. He believes in reparations. Mira doesn't disagree: she has no alternate vision of the world to compete with his.

She only wishes he wouldn't get interested in a different woman every day.

I mean, look at him even now: he can't stop glancing at that woman one table over, the one who is still FaceTiming with the screechy child. The woman is bringing to her mouth a huge forkful of tortellini, dripping tomato sauce and cheese, pointing at it, opening her mouth wide — for the benefit of the girl, apparently: Look how big of a bite I'm going to take! She is wearing golden earrings in the shape of feathers, and a spotless, cream-coloured silk blouse. The blouse is iridescent, difficult to look away from: it undulates with the beauty of an ocean at dusk, one gentle wave. Mira admires this: ordering a dish with red sauce and eating it freely, while wearing an impeccable, light-coloured silk blouse.

Bernard turns back to Mira. "Are you seeing that friend of yours here?"

Just then an enormous pizza lands a couple of tables over, slides out so far that the platter knocks a little boy on the chest. He laughs uncertainly, stuck between hurt and delight.

"I said, are you seeing—"

"Oh, I don't know."

"You were how old when you left over there? You haven't seen him since?"

"About twenty years I haven't seen him. Something like that. He left for France when I was already in Canada. You lost track of people back then. You'd hear so and so was in such and such a place, then someone would say, no, that was last year, now they're in Finland or Australia or something."

"Hm."

Twenty years must seem a long time to Bernard.

"I almost forgot—your grandma asked about you."

He puts down his slice.

"How's she doing?"

"Her TV's broke."

"A broken television—it's like a problem from the 1980s!"

The woman FaceTiming does an unselfconscious dramatization of kiss blowing and kiss catching and hiding the kiss inside her cheek and blowing that same kiss out her mouth by popping the ballooned cheek with her finger.

"The TV's actually a big problem."

"Is it?" He half-turns and half-smiles in the direction of the woman.

"Yes. It's the only thing she—are you listening?"

"What do you mean am I listening? I'm right here."

"It's the only thing she does. She doesn't like the neighbours, so hardly anyone—"

"We can get her a new television, right?"

"She might expect you to know how to fix it."

"Very funny. But really, how is she feeling?"

The girl inside the iPhone squeals, makes kissing noises, au revoir, au revoir, and finally the woman swipes the screen, puts her phone face down, and swigs the remnant of her wine.

Then she turns to them and says, in English, "That is my niece. I talk to her on FaceTime every night."

Mira is horrified that they've been caught staring, but Bernard, not missing a beat, says, "She looks so sweet."

"Oh, she has the biggest heart," the young woman says, shaking her head with its long dark hair, which is as smooth and light-catching as her blouse. She extends her hands as if she were taking a giant gorilla into a hug. "Just a monster heart. Almost no friends though. Only at the hospital."

She sits at the edge of her chair, as if about to leave, but she keeps talking.

The niece is one of a dozen, but, the woman will admit, her favourite.

She accepts wine Bernard offers from the half-litre jug he and Mira have been sharing.

"I was too young when the other nieces and nephews were born, and they lived far away, but Isabelle — man, it was like they'd injected steroids into my heart!"

"How old were you?"

"When she was born? Twenty-two."

"Almost like me when Bernard came along." Mira blushes as she says it — what the heck?

"He's your favourite, isn't he?"

"No, I'm just the only one. She can't choose."

Mira's tired, but can't bring herself to leave. It's partly that she finds the young woman oddly compelling, with her forthrightness and poise, but mostly that she's figuring out — what on earth is Bebe doing?

Not until the wine jug is nearly empty and their plates cleared does Mira admit to herself she's really superfluous here.

You dolt, she scolds herself. You hanger-on.

"Would you take this for the pigeon?" says Bernard, as she rises to leave. He has saved his crusts, and she puts them in her purse.

It could make for a triumphant text to her sister, so invested in Bernard moving on: Bernard doing well. Chatting up attractive Parisian, very expectedly chic.

But maybe not so triumphant if she includes the other attractive Parisians: so many of them, in so few hours!

When she walks alone back to the hotel there are few souls on the streets, only lamplight, and the same faint breeze as earlier in the evening when they set out for the restaurant. Rather like the night before, her time with Bernard has ended before it's hardly begun. When he was a boy, she played chasing games with him beyond her endurance, for the sake of his glee; she took him to playgrounds and nature centres and kid plays even when David would rather have spent the day in bed with her; she booked days off work to get him out of the house when Ljilja worked and Dennis could not manage putting on shoes; she has been gentle with him when he was grumpy, whiny, and difficult, whether a toddler or a teenager; she opened her doors to him and Aisha when they seemed to need it. So what?

She feels the very distant building of tears, again, and pushes them back, because this recurring weepiness, recently and mysteriously developed, is more shameful to her than her nightly ruminating.

For no clear reason she sees Bernard standing by a window, making himself sick waiting for Aisha; and she grasps, finally, stupidly, what he's been doing here: a tour of the Bernard and Aisha Paris, the glory of their last summer, pre-shocking-phone-pictures-of-naked-veterinarians. Thus the pizzeria tonight, and of course the hotel. Getting the same room he'd had with Aisha was precisely the coincidence he'd aimed himself toward. The surprise is only that he agreed to switch rooms when the coincidence materialized.

And what was he doing now? The Bernard she had shaped from his childhood and even from his unusually candid confidences must be a true picture — but incomplete, at least.

He might be hoping for help from her: he might think that she, having twenty-some years on him, has clues about what you do with your past. Embarrassingly, she only knows it accumulates, and the accumulation gathers speed and momentum. And what kind of wisdom was that?

She reaches the corner of Rue Du Sommerard, where there is a small, fine line outline of a horse done in black paint, high up on the wall of a building, a horse in flight, thin-limbed and fragile, a thing she's noticed each time she's walked by it in the last two days. A small thing she's come to love, she realizes, for no clear reason, except perhaps the unlikeliness of its existence.

No, Bernard is probably not hoping for anything from her. He's travelling with her because he doesn't want to arrive at his grandmother's place alone and struggle with the inevitable awkwardness. And he's visiting his grandmother mostly because he's meeting his friends in Italy, and it would look bad if he were so close and didn't go see her. He does have a bit of a guilt complex. No, she won't text Ljilja about Bernard's unexpected romances. Romances, how old fashioned of her to call them that. Hookups! Is that what they call them?

And she grasps something else. As if she were approaching a shore, and the objects on it — black weeds on the rocks, say, and prickly grasses, and stone houses and olive trees — have finally come clearly into view, she sees that Mirko is not going to write back to her even if he has seen her message. As for the home address she has, it matches his last name and first initial, but it may not be his at all. And anyway, does she have it in her to knock uninvited on a door behind which may be a stranger, of one kind or another?

As often in her life, great expectations shift into a countdown to the end. Tomorrow is the third day in Paris, the last full day, and then the real business of life will continue.

THE LIGHT IS ON in the dining room. Sitting at one of the tables, with paperwork spread out in front of her, is the woman with white hair and black eyebrows, the one who broke the smile chain with the Americans at breakfast. Mira nods when the woman looks up.

"Di vam je sin?"

Where is your son? Mira is startled, then about to answer, He's still out, charming yet another young woman. Then she catches the fact that Bernard is not her son.

"Nephew," she says, in Croatian, smiling and shaking her head. "Staying out late."

"Ah." The woman takes off the glasses attached to a thin chain hanging on her neck and rubs her eyes.

Amazing how you can recognize a peer. Mira knows immediately that they are of the same generation, give or take a year, from a similar town and even of a similar schooling. What is it that you recognize, when you recognize such a thing? The face exactly as aged as yours? The glasses and eye-rubbing?

"I was hoping I'd see one of you, because there's a little problem with your room. You don't need to worry — just a toilet leak below, and they've had to go into your suite to get to the pipe."

"Is there damage?"

"No, no."

Mira remembers the pigeon.

"Room 612?" Bernard's room, then.

"Yes. You can have a cup of tea or coffee with me while they finish up, if you like?"

Mira accepts the tea and sits down. The dining room is warm and warmly lit, with hints of the disorder of home: plants on the windowsill, not all thriving; knick-knacks once intended for some indefinite folksy aesthetic effect — mini-cacti growing in faux-pail pots — but now taken over by other, unintentionally homey-looking stuff, like dull pencils, scribbled-on pads of paper, and tubes of hand cream. She'd rather stay because her heart is a foolish organ, relentlessly padding about for its comfort, even when Mira herself thinks it has learned its lesson.

The woman calls out from the kitchen. "Is it your first time in Paris?"

"Yes," Mira yells. Not the one I would've imagined, but here we are.

The woman walks back to the table and sets down a glass jar of honey, two spoons, and two oranges. Her hair is fine, even white, smoothly parted down the middle, styled to curl below the ear. The oranges are an appealing surprise to Mira.

"I'm Merima," she says. Around her neck is a gold chain with two letter pendants, *A* and *B*. "I'll be back with the tea." She leaves and returns in a minute with two mugs, just faintly steaming.

"Rosehip," she says, when she puts them down.

Mira stirs in a spoon of thick, dark amber honey.

"What a beauty," she says.

"I bring jars of this every time I go home for a visit. My father kept bees near Mostar, and now my brother's gone back and started the operation again. I'm sorry I don't have anything to offer for a snack, but I thought you might like an orange, now or to bring to your room. Well. And how do you like the city?"

How does she like the city, indeed. What is the city? Can it be summed up by the feeling a stranger has, an ignorant stranger like her, while walking through it?

"I liked the park today. I mean Luxembourg Gardens. I spent the morning just sitting there. I liked how people simply sat there, surrounded by all those flowers. I can imagine the effort of planting and maintaining those flowers."

"I like the gardens too. I go there if I can catch more than a fifteen-minute break here. I like the fountains."

It's excessive, but Mira stirs another spoonful of honey into her tea.

"How long have you lived here?"

"Nearly twenty years."

"Has Paris changed since then?"

"To be honest, I can't remember much from when I first arrived. I didn't notice things like gardens or monuments. I didn't feel Paris as a real place, a place that had meaning, that I could walk in and be a person in, if you know what I mean?"

Mira takes an orange, punctures the skin at the top with her nail.

"I should have cut those, at least, shouldn't I have — well, you know, one thing you were excused from, briefly, back then, was having any purpose in your present life. We complained of flats that had reliable radiators but poor water pressure, flats without balconies and those with a spot of garden where you might grow some potatoes and beans. It didn't occur to anyone to even go walking in the city. I know some people back home envied me, imagining some connection between my having studied French and being now in Paris — as if I'd got a scholarship to study at the Sorbonne or something. Complete nonsense! My French was weak and awkward. In any case, I was only looking for others like me. People I could look at to remind me of who I am."

"Were there many?"

"Some, not that many. I'd walk by the Serb cafés just to hear some familiar music — but there was a lot of hate then, of course, and this mix of familiarity and sudden, profound strangeness was unsettling to me. And at the little apartment I lived in, I tried for days to stretch dough for pita, but it didn't stretch right. The pan stuck, the oven I couldn't adjust. So I gave up and just ate French loafs and butter all the time."

The banal troubles of the immigrant. Flour is not what it should be, the eggs have pale yolks, even the sugar is not really sugar.

"Gosh, my trouble in Canada was not finding any good bread. I'd have given anything for a real French loaf then! And some decent homemade jam to spread on it."

"Your nephew's name is Bernard, isn't it? My son is also Bernard. That's why I thought it a fun coincidence at first, thinking the young man was your son. Do you have children?"

Thus the *B* pendant around her neck, thinks Mira.

"No."

"I have two sons, actually. One I was pregnant with when I came here."

She pauses here, for emphasis, clearly. "Can you imagine? His father stayed in Bosnia. We had married young, which upset my parents, who had spent their whole lives as parents being so-called liberal so that I might finish university before becoming married and pregnant, and there I was, twenty-two, announcing my wedding plans! And I won, I got married, and when the war came, my father said, what will you do now — what side can you be on? And my mother said, nonsense, as always there are only two paths, that of the righteous people and that of the rest, and Merima and Boro are both on the path of the righteous. Which at the time I took solace in and which strikes me now as both true and not. My father said then, that is right, but this is only the beginning of how they will estrange us from one another."

The peel of the orange is stubborn and coming off only in small pieces, and Mira has barely got through a quarter of it. "So you came here pregnant — and alone?"

"Yes. And being not really welcome in my apartment, I spent most days in a pathetic café down the street, reading and re-reading Danilo Kiš's writings from Paris."

Mira remembers, vaguely, the writer's *Encyclopaedia of the Dead*. But the only thing she really remembers well about Kiš is something she must've read in a biography, or an interview. He'd lost a lung to cancer, and describing the loss afterwards, he said something like, "When I used to say *my soul*, I'd tap my chest, like this; now when I put my hand there, that side is empty." A man missing a part of himself: an organ, something invisible, something one can in fact live without, yet is still mysteriously dear.

"But one day I forgot the book on the table of a café and when I went back the next day the waiter said, What book? I went back when different waiters were on shift, until they all recognized me as the woman who keeps asking after the same missing object, and finally they told me not to return. I was devastated, because it proved that both objects and people were easily and permanently lost. There was no sense to it — just randomness and coincidence: who's working the check-point when you're trying to escape, who picks up a book and trashes it. I think now the waiters had been tired of me sitting there day after day, with a single drink, looking very pregnant and forlorn."

Mira also clearly remembers how she held on to things — the small stack of books she moved with her from one flat to another, the gold chain around her neck.

"When I lived in Zagreb during the war," she says, "I did the same thing, sat in a café with one coffee for hours. No one cared, of course. No one was spending money then, or almost no one. For a few months I lived in this very dank, half-basement apartment in one of those turn-of-the-century buildings in the centre — those tiny dwellings for railway men, you know? Ten square metres with a bathroom. And stone walls half a metre thick. I shared it with this woman, a distant relation who took me in. She was a seamstress, and her Singer machine and her fabrics took up most of the space. The thing is, she had problems no one had mentioned to me: she believed the fabrics had their own desires for how they might be cut, and should she not follow their wishes, they might get into mischief."

"Goodness! And what did she imagine the mischief to be?"

"The worst one was that the fabrics would smother her. And when these delusions took over, she became frightened and cagey, accusing me of having moved things secretly. She also argued with her clients, because she sometimes made strange alterations to their pants and dresses. I felt sorry for her, because she was unwell and could hardly make a living, and, it seemed to me, she was likely to die alone and afraid in that place that already resembled a cold tomb. But every night I had to fall asleep — or try to — to the sound of her muttering, and I was increasingly worried that she might indeed smother me in my sleep as she feared her silks and cottons would smother her!"

Mira had not been afraid of destitution, nor even of violence, as much as of this stagnant, rotten atmosphere, like a faint, ever-present undertone of rot or feces. So she bolted from there even before she had anywhere else to live. She is about to tell Merima how, to get a different dwelling, this one at least bright and warm, she had taken up with a man — a slightly sly, cheerily opportunistic man — but she pulls back, for the familiar shame that rises up.

"How did you end up in Canada?"

"It was a few years after that. My sister went first, and because she married — pretty quickly — a Canadian citizen, and because of the war, she managed to get me across."

Merima says, "For everyone, if they live long enough, there will be a before and after: something will cut into their life. For us, I suppose, everything is after the war. After leaving the country. But since that break, I've realized you can have several *after*s. Each time that your timeline is split yet again, you have to start from scratch. You have to dig up something you didn't know you had in you. Improvise a new way to be."

Mira considers the orange, now half-peeled and messy-looking. Her fingers are sticky and sweet-smelling. She looks up. "Do you think, then, that each *after* is like a rehearsal, a practice run for the final *after*?"

"Death, you mean?"

"Say you cut an orange in half, then cut the second half into quarters, then cut the quarter in half — now you've just got one eighth, because the other parts are in the *before* category. And maybe you can split that eighth again, but eventually you can't, you can't cut that sliver in half because it's just a mess, and there's hardly anything there at all."

The front door of the hotel opens and closes.

"Have you ever wanted to move back?" Mira says, somewhat urgently.

"Move back?" Merima laughs. "Oh no. In my second life, you see, I married a Frenchman, a real fourth-generation Parisian, if you can believe that. Our son is Bernard. Can I show you a picture?"

Merima pulls out her wallet, from a purse hanging on the chair, and takes out a posed school portrait of a boy with a goofy wink and hair made to stand up in spikes. He is fresh-faced, with a sweet, upturned nose.

Mira looks for a long moment, getting over her disappointment at this turn in the conversation. But when she finally says, "He's magical," she means it, he is.

"Well, yes." Merima laughs. "He transformed me."

Under the open arch of the dining room entrance appears the young man who works here, whom Mira suspects of being high all the time. He has long hair covering the sides of his face and Merima looks startled to see him. They speak a quick, lively exchange in French.

Mira sees how Merima's hand casually hangs over the picture of the boy, partially covering it.

"I'm afraid it's time for me to go home," she says, looking suddenly vulnerable, like a person woken up too early.

Mira looks from one to the other and realizes that this boy is Merima's son too, the son who was still inside her when she arrived here. She hadn't noticed any resemblance earlier, and he looks younger than he must be, but she's sure of it, regardless. There is a current in the room — of guilt, reproach, longing — that comes from a history unknown to her.

Mira rises. "Thank you for the tea." It's a weak thing to say, and she's further disappointed by this conclusion.

"Yes. I'm sure your room is fine now."

Mira looks down at the mess of orange peel and the uneaten yet tarnished fruit.

"Don't worry about that," Merima says, following her eyes. "I'll throw it out for you."

"Oh no, don't clean up after me." She begins to gather the bits of peel in one hand, dropping some on the chair and the floor.

Merima picks up the cups and the good orange. "Really," she says.

Mira's got most of the peels squished inside her fist now and she takes the orange in her other hand. She waves at Merima awkwardly, not sure if she's waving away the help or waving goodbye.

There is no garbage basket she can see, so she climbs up the stairs holding everything tightly in her hands. In the room, she dumps the peel, but can't decide about the orange and sets it down on the tiny table against the wall. She leans over the pigeon's box, sees the small dark bulk of the bird, its eyes closed, its daily bread eaten.

She sits on the floor next to be box. Sleep would not come to her, you could just tell that sort of thing. Finding Merima in the dining room, bent over paperwork, that warm light on, reminded her of her own mother, who was also a hotel manager, at the better of the two hotels in town, and often worked late at the kitchen table. Mira would walk home from school, when class was held in the evening shift, and come in from the outside darkness to find her mom in the yellow glow of the kitchen bulb, sheets of plans spread out in front of her — often frowning, sometimes getting on the telephone. "You didn't iron the tablecloths," Mira would hear her saying, "so you must come in early tomorrow. That's right, before seven." God forbid there be a wedding, and there were weddings all the time.

Once Mira was arriving home with a composition she was proud of, a rare thing. She was not great in history, okay in math, short of excellent in what was then Serbo-Croatian language. Their composition subjects made much use of the seasons: spring in my town, winter in my town, what I love about autumn. She had written of buying roast chestnuts from the vendor by the newsstand on the square. You walk up, it's a foggy evening, the vendor is friendly, hello girl with the purple scarf! He rolls up the newsprint into a cone, swish, his hands are blackened, the scoop descends on the roasted pile in the metal bin, they slide in, tumbling, their shells softly knocking against each other, a second scoop, a little extra for this sweet girl. They steam, only for a few seconds, they smell smoky and metallic and sweet.

She added some things about the fog and the yellow leaves fluttering to the ground, which was the expected fare for the autumn composition. Her teacher, who was not a smiling sort, had half-smiled when handing it to her, and written words of praise — "very good details." Mira walked home in the dark, and as usual, there was the warm kitchen light, the glow from the television Ljilja was watching in the other room, the smell of roasting yams, Mom at the kitchen table. After taking off her things and going to the bathroom, Mira sat next to her, inching a kitchen chair a little too close. Her mother also smelled warm, like the kitchen; and there was, as always, an undertone of perfume, very faint, from a bottle Mira can still picture, a triangular glass beast.

"Look," Mira said eventually, holding her notebook, spread open to the relevant page.

"Yes? Oh. Yes, you got a good grade, I see. Finally. Hm." She took the notebook into her hands. "Your *b*'s — look here — your *b*'s are still crooked. You have to practice that. Your *l*'s are better, see? It's because you worked on them so much. Here" — her mom reached for a pencil — "find your practicing notebook and just do a page before dinner. Have you washed your hands?"

Of course Mira had washed her hands. Her mom got up to fetch her a plate of yams and boiled chicken, and Mira obligingly reached into her backpack for the practicing notebook. As she started writing her *b*'s, lining up the tops to the top line, her mom sprinkled cinnamon on the yams and it overrode the faint smell of perfume.

You can have several afters, Merima had said. Was she talking about her own life after marrying her Parisian, having her baby Bernard? She didn't say whether her first husband was alive. Well, Mira was in her second *after*, in any case. She got lucky the first time. But — she could get lucky again, like Merima did? Mirko, even, really still could call. He could be on the fence, busy with something until this very night, when he's planning to call and say, I'm so glad I caught you while you're still here. Life has been crazy, but I'd love to see you. Yes, she would say, yes, I do know the café with the green satin chairs by the Luxembourg Gardens — yes, see you there tomorrow morning! Stranger things have happened. Life could still sweep her up.

IN FRONT OF the hotel, the long-haired dude — night-duty manager? — is smoking a joint. He waves at Bernard as Bernard goes inside. Instead of upstairs, he walks into the dining room; he's hoping for juice, or pop, something sweet to settle his stomach. There, sitting at a table with a deck of cards in front of her, is the American girl. She's built a small card tower, and when Bernard stops to look at her, she blushes. He moves on to the kitchen, to the fridge, finds nothing good, starts opening cupboards. Where do they keep the juice? They serve them juice every morning. He'd like some sugar in any form. Jam packets? He turns back to look at the girl, sitting there in her sweatshirt, head propped up on her hand, now dismantling the tower card by card and decidedly not looking at him. She's got a bottle of Coke on the table, nearly full. How did he not see that?

"Hi. I'm sorry, this is weird, but — do you think I could — I'm staying here at the hotel too, and I was just looking for something sweet to drink — do you think I could have some of your Coke?"

"Some of my Coke?"

"I mean just a little, I'd bring a glass of course."

The remainder of the tower falls, and she winces. Looks up at him. Blames him, clearly, for the collapse.

"I'm sorry to interrupt you —"

"So bring a glass."

He does — he finds the glasses stacked neatly lip-down on the counter. She's about to pour when she stops and says, "I've already drunk from it. I mean, germs and all."

"Oh God, that's fine, that's totally fine."

It fizzes, foams, and he downs it before the foam has settled. Delightful.

"Here, have more."

He sits across from her.

"Are you sure?"

"Like, it's Coke."

"I don't know why it's so good right now."

"Are you alright?"

"What do you mean?"

"I just thought your hands were shaking. Sorry."

"Oh no." He puts the cup down, puts his hands under the table. She refills his glass.

He's just come from walking Selma home. It's not far from here, she'd said, as they were leaving the pizza place. It was raining lightly, and they were having a fine time; she was funny, he liked her, and he thought she must like him too, because they were doing a lot of the nudging and arm-grazing people do when they want to find a way to touch each other. In fact, he'd just got to gently draping his arm over her shoulder and she'd reached over and pressed her palm into the small of his back.

So they'd just got to that fine point, when, out of nowhere, in front of them on the sidewalk, out stepped this woman, this apparent lover of Selma's, as it would turn out, a striking woman in a sleeveless white shirt and a short shag of blond hair. She was nearly as tall as him and her shoulders were muscular and beautiful: a swimmer, he thought? She wore no jacket and carried no umbrella, and her arms and clavicles and shoulders glistened with the rain.

It was as if by stepping in front of them she stepped onto a stage; the register exploded, and they were in an opera. She was beseeching. She cupped her hands as if holding a precarious handful of water, or berries; then she brought the handful to her heart, then opened her arms wide as if throwing, letting scatter, whatever it was she had held so gingerly.

It would have been laughable, except that he could really see the tiny strawberries flying, getting bruised and destroyed on the ground.

Selma seemed furious at the sudden appearance. She was actually stomping her foot in anger, her large block heel as loud as a hammer. Even so, the woman continued: she turned her hands palms up and ran her forefinger over the length of each finger of her left hand. He'd never seen anyone do that before. When she then took a step toward Selma, Selma put out her arm to keep her at a distance. For the first time in the scene, Bernard wondered if Selma was afraid and he stepped in closer to her. In that moment, also for the first time, the woman looked at him — thinking, what, I could knock him down in a hot minute? Selma shook and shook her finger, and boy, she yelled, a torrential outpour. And as the yelling crescendoed, the woman's face, her straight jaw, her beautiful mouth, collapsed into a quivering sob. You should have seen it, Bernard said, in his mind, to Aisha. She started to punch her own chest and shoulder. But limply, like she didn't really have it in her, like the opera was now in its sad pathetic part, where the hero has maybe just enough energy to die. Selma quieted and took a step forward. With one hand, she grasped the woman's wrist, and with her other arm she held her in a strange half-embrace.

Oddly, though he should have understood some of their French, though they yelled as much as they stomped and gestured, afterwards he couldn't remember a thing they'd said. The whole scene was a mute drama.

He downs the second glass of Coke Alice has poured for him. Alice has her hair up in one of those cute, messy half-ponytails he's seen Aisha and other girlfriends use when they were, say, studying at home in their sweatshirts.

"So what are you doing in Paris, anyway?" he asks.

"I don't know. Just hanging out, I guess. It was my parents' idea. Is that your mom you're with?"

"Oh, no. My aunt."

The manager guy walks back in, goes to sit behind the desk.

Alice keeps looking at Bernard like she's waiting for an explan-ation. Instead, he says, "Your parents seem nice."

She shrugs, then tilts her head and pulls on the elastic to free her hair.

"Well, and what are you doing in Paris?"

Should he say, I wanted to see if I could uncover my own small possibilities for destruction? I wanted to see if you really can enter the same river twice, since my counselor said you couldn't? Mostly I wanted to see if I should try to get my girl-friend back. Or if I even truly want her back. Not that she's available or anything.

"Just sightseeing for a few days. We're going on to Croatia, then Italy. I mean, I'm going to Italy. My grandma lives in Croatia, and she's kind of sick."

At the word sick, he feels a shift in the atmosphere, in Alice's downcast eyes, and he remembers her mom is likely still recovering. Or maybe not recovering.

Alice collects a few of the cards, which are still all over the table, but half-heartedly, as if it's not entirely worth it to try.

He had reluctantly let Selma go; she was tired, and apolo-getic, but, she reassured him, safe. She'd call him tomorrow if he wanted to get together. He said he did, though he didn't. And he didn't think she'd call, either.

But Alice — why is Alice sitting here alone, drinking Coke, building stupid card towers?

She's sad, he can see it. And when he's sad, he hates being alone. Alice's thin blondish hair has enough electricity in it that it sticks to her temples and cheeks, and she has to keep moving it out of the way. The yellow light of the room shines on her head, on her runaway hair, on her pale fingers, and she is a sunlit child, a glowing woman in a pensive interior, a plump bird on a barren branch, unprepared for the winter that will carry away things it hardly knew it needed so much. Love is an impulse that can be turned toward many a creature. And sex a shortcut, a tumble through uncleared wilderness, but soft, soft shrubs, wildflowers, fuzzy grasses, and suddenly you were right there, in a brighter clearing, or maybe a darker tangle of trees — in what, regardless, looked like the heart of things.

"What is your grandma sick with?" she says.

"She had a stroke. A mini-stroke. I mean, she's old, and we worry about her."

He understands Alice is disappointed in a specific and understandable way, and he sees, also, that she is still holding on, regardless.

"Do you like card tricks?" she says.

"As much as I like card towers, yes. No, I know one single card trick."

"I could show you some good ones, but" — she looks toward the manager sitting at reception — "I think they probably don't want us sitting around here all night."

The guy at reception looks as if he would hardly raise his head if a whole crowd came in with balloons and piñatas. But it's easy enough for Bernard to say, and not feel slimy about it, I guess we could go upstairs.

In his room, sitting on his bed, she shows him, for real, some good card tricks, which he watches lying on his side, head propped up on his elbow. Then, without a word, she moves the cards aside and just stretches out her body, along the length of his, tucking in her head near his elbow. When he puts his head down to join her, when he leans into it, he feels her not quite shaking, but vibrating, just perceptibly.

She will fall asleep and the vibrating will stop. He will sleep in spurts, thinking, each time he wakes yet again, I should never have had that Coke. He will dream, or remember, sleeping next to his mom, the faint trace of fruity lotion on her skin, the soft roundness of her triceps, which he would press his palm to as he fell asleep. How he only fell half-asleep if she wasn't there at bedtime, and never missed the sound of her at the door, later, sometimes very late, and the comforting sounds of the things she did after she got in, the scrape of her shoes being laid on the ground and pushed in toward the wall, the water running in the bathroom and the slight knock of the toothbrush against the plastic cup, and eventually the click of the bathroom light switch, the happiest sound, for then she would open the bedroom door and quietly move the comforter back, and check with her hand very gently to see where he is, and he wouldn't usually let on he's awake, but he'd rustle and move and find her arm and hold and breathe her in and then truly, peacefully fall asleep.

He wakes again. A distorted wave-rectangle of light falls over Alice's elbow and hip. She's very calm in sleep. Is it very bad to just want to sleep next to a person, even if it's a person you'll never get to know?

In the room next door, last summer, he and Aisha had set their little digital camera on the table and aimed it at the bed, where they had sex, which looked surprisingly good on video when they watched later, even though everyone tells you it will look stupid. And then later that same day, Aisha accidentally erased the video, when they were at the Musée d'Orsay, as she was freeing up room to take more pictures of the paintings. They thought they would make another, but they didn't. He tucks in a little closer to Alice. Her hair is still full of static and he touches an electrified strand by her ear very gently with his fingertips.

MIRA TRIES TO CONNECT to the internet, but the connection fails again and again. She hears someone's late-night shower down the hall. It's as if she's hearing David showering, in the master bathroom. She'd sleep in an extra half hour and the pleasant ping-ping of the water would transition her into wakefulness. When the ping-ping stopped, it was time to rise. She'd always come into the bathroom just as he was toweling off. She pictures his legs: softly hairy, with curly, lamb-like hair, all the way up to his thighs. Then the nail on his left big toe, permanently damaged from years of sports. After his shower, he would comb his hair into a slick, exaggerated wave, gleeful at the ridiculousness of it; then he would sit on the lounge chair in the living room, wrapped in a towel held together at the waist, reading news on his laptop and telling her funny and infuriating bits. He might keep both an espresso cup and a tall glass of juice balanced on the arm of that chair. He tended to balance cups in precarious places: steering the car with one hand and taking sips from his open coffee cup with the other.

She liked the small cheerful risk of it. The coffee sloshed but never spilled. In the early years of their marriage, sitting in the armchair, in that post-shower glow, he seemed optimistic: freshly shaven, enjoying his good-looking body, scheming possibilities — for the afternoon, the weekend, their undefined life.

Her youth had been interrupted by calamity, but on these mornings, there was no trace of the rupture. They were just a young married couple, looking for good-enough jobs, buying IKEA odds and ends, trying out new cocktails with their friends.

We who've seen the early season potential of our childhood exhausted. Lines she's read come to her unbidden, without context, like these images of past life. *First caffeine of the morning when our lives were surely past noon.*

The shower down the hall ends and she hears quiet steps and gentle creaks; a whisper of voices as a door opens and closes. Her phone alerts her to messages, but it's only a work email and a text from Ljilja that says, *Haven't got a hold of Mom yet — she must be getting out for her walks again. Those floods across the border are crazy. I hope it won't get bad at home. Dennis got a beautiful shot of a male orca when we went whale watching, I'll get him to send it to you. What have you two got planned for the last day in Paris?*

She wants to talk to Ljilja, but right now this does not feel like an urgent text to answer. She tells herself, Have another cup of tea.

But there's no kettle, of course, and no tea.

Whatever else she might have imagined about love or its dissolution or her own future, it was not the sudden flattening of everything that took place after David left. The whole house took on the sad, undramatic pallor of poverty and temporary dwellings, the dustiness of a bus depot waiting room. The same dullness of the many different spare rooms she had lived in during the war. Who can wait to get out of such a place? Everyone knows it's nowhere to expect anything. This pathetic colour spread to the books she loved, written, after all, for distant people and for distant purposes, which she had mistakenly imbued with her own desires. It spread to her coffee mugs, the bread and jam she ate for breakfast, the houseplants and the curtains, the streets she drove down, the cashiers at the supermarket. Ditto the neighbours. Ditto her friends, who had no great wisdom after all.

And ditto, finally, her own body, the most shameful transformation. How perishable it was: her skin grown thin, eyelids creased, hands irreparably dry. Ordinary flesh. She would never regain the innocent belief that someone sitting next to her in the movie theatre found her physical proximity acceptable rather than odious.

Everything, in short, returned to physical, unholy matter. No: neither holy nor sinful. Simply finite.

Maybe she shouldn't have been surprised by this, but she was. And one day when she dropped in on Ljilja's place and saw Bernard, already as tall as now, sitting in front of the giant flat-screen television, arguing with a friend over the verisimilitude of a new version of a video game, she thought, So that's what everything has amounted to. Where was the use?

And she had to move in this strange world, acting as if she recognized everything. But, actually, the worse part was that she did. The delusion had been the brief belief in having got beyond the purgatory of the waiting room.

If every *after* was indeed not a rehearsal for death, nor a narrowing of life until there was nothing left to lose, was it then the opposite — enriching? Was each *after* an expansion, because you had to reinvent all the stuff, like eating and walking and friendship and love? But you still had to find a place for all the weird dead stuff of your old life in this new world. And did the new creation make up for the loss? Because you wouldn't be in the after if you hadn't left behind something big. Did things just even out, a gain for a loss?

Was there any sense in trying to conceive of this as an equation?

Through the wall behind the bed, the same room next door from which she heard noise last night, now comes the sound of an argument. The talking is loud enough that she can make out that it's French, which she has no hope of understanding. It's a woman's voice, and though it quiets again, Mira picks up on both the tone and rhythm: a deliberate, staccato rhythm, the tone sharp and attacking. It's as if the woman were spitting out a well-rehearsed list of transgressions.

Mira readjusts her pillow, sinks deeper into it. She thinks, maybe the trouble was that she'd tried to make David every-thing — a husband, a mother, a father, a country, a child, a lover, a home. When he suggested they see a counselor, she'd felt betrayed — how could they need another person, a stranger? Maybe that was a fundamental sort of mistake. A really kind of stupid delusion. And David, being just a human, and will-ing to be a husband and lover, tired of being perceived a fail-ure for not manifesting as a deity with ten fleshly and abstract incarnations.

Clatter from next door, like someone trying again and again to close a faulty closet door.

Then a short silence, then a different voice, a child's voice, speaking briefly, as if offering an explanation. Wrong thing to do, apparently, because it prompts the woman's monologue to start up again. Now it sounds even more vigorous, with deliberate enunciations, punched out repetitions; warning, reproaching, accusing?

Mira flips around, puts the pillow at the foot of the bed, to get away from this argument. In any case, what was the use of having, say, such an insight about one's stupid delusion, now? When the divorce papers have been safely put away. Always this gap between the physical manifestation of life and your understanding of it. What you understood or imagined about life and what was actually taking place were just two separate tracks. Maybe they connected sometimes, but you certainly couldn't call it a tango, a beautiful harmony of two dancers.

It was a mismatch of space and time. Like misplaced objects — they exist, you know they are sitting somewhere, innocent, ready to serve their purpose, capable of fulfilling your desires, but they are not here now, and the reality of your need is now. Why the gap? Was the failed bridge always a limited human consciousness? Or is the consciousness itself an expression of the flow of time, the true, un-synced flow of time?

Even with her head at the foot of the bed, she can hear the cycle from next door repeat several times: silence, then the timid child's voice, then the drone voice again, relentless, for minutes on end. It's almost worse from the slight distance of the other side of the bed, because it's more a purely sinister undertone: no language for one to latch on to, just a visceral hostility. Impossible this can keep going on. Impossible the child deserves such torment.

It quiets after a while, and then there is a long silence. She begins to drift.

She's talking to David, in the basement of their house, about windows. He wants to put in new windows, big ones. She's standing with her arms crossed, saying, It's too much money. I don't like basements. I wish we didn't have this dark cavern under our lives all the time.

She has to pee, but each time she tries, she can't get there — first the toilet is just a sculpture of a toilet, and then strangely tall people are gathered round it and she knows she'll never get through. She hears laughter, tinkling and happy. Then a murmur of voices that gets louder, and then there is a door opening — she could swear it is Bernard's — and she floats to the hallway, which is all padded in a kind of red velvet, on the floor and the walls and the ceiling, and she sees the young French woman, who smiles as Bernard holds the door narrowly opened from the inside; after few quick words in a strange language, the door closes, the woman brings up her hand to adjust her messy bun, and then she is off, an absurdly large white purse slung with the strap across the open collar of her still-flawless blouse. The girl looks brisk and self-possessed, off to her job, no doubt, her mind already on the next thing, on the day ahead, where she will be a bit tired but otherwise keeping it together, well-dressed, used to life offering spontaneous pleasures that carry with them a slight lack of sleep.

The soft clip of her footsteps on the stairs recedes, and recedes, and it is growing fainter for a long time. Mira opens her eyes. She is still in bed. The light in the room seems ambiguous — is it really morning? Her body is a bag of wet sand thrown onto the bed. Is the window open? The covers smell like wind.

WHEN MIRA HAS willed herself to move, she looks through the patio door and sees a slightly pink sky, a clean dawn — barely morning. She has a fierce need to pee. Afterwards, she walks down the hall in flip-flops, to shower, past the door of the room bordering hers; she pauses next to it, but now hears nothing, as if no one were in there at all.

What an exhausting night. She feels pummeled. She is about to enter the shower room when someone opens the door from the inside — the American girl, stepping out, the girl whom she'd taken for a teenager, who looks now actually more like a twelve-year-old, plump and ignorant, an oversized toddler. Mira has been mystified by such people most of her life, grownups untouched by adulthood.

But as the girl exits and passes by her, their eyes meet and Mira thinks, suddenly, she is wrong.

Then the door of Bernard's room opens and he calls softly, "Alice," in the same, too-late instant that he sees Mira in the hallway.

She continues into the shower room without turning back — what else? — as if she has not heard or seen anything. Start again, she thinks, as she turns on the shower. Is it morning? Yes. The girl's name is Alice? Must be. Bernard was calling Alice. Alice was showering. Alice was showering in the bathroom on their floor, which is not the floor her room is on. Alice was showering after — seriously?

But the French girl? Could there have been the French girl and Alice? For the love of God, Bebe. Was there really a French girl? Yes — at the restaurant, anyway: she had listened to her talk for an hour! She looked as slick in the morning as she had in the evening. But then she remembers the red velvet walls, and herself, floating, wondering at her invisibility.

After showering — which, frankly, is again a bit of unpleasant business, because, as expected, there are indeed a few strands of hair in some unmissable spot — she wraps herself tightly in the hotel's stiff, over-bleached towel and goes to stand on the balcony. It is cold, she shivers, but day is breaking open and she wants to see it. She's spent the last twenty years in the fog of the beginning of life, the illusion that whatever life meant, whatever relevance it would hold, was just getting going. As if all the life she'd had before running away to Canada didn't even count. To have acknowledged it does count would have meant accepting that she lost it — whatever it might have led to.

What a sleight of hand she played on herself! But now she sees the shadows that say, It is well past noon, a lazy but advancing afternoon. The most enduringly frightening story-book of her childhood was of a girl who thought she always had time: she stayed in bed too long, slowly ate her breakfast, and didn't listen to her mother's warning that she should not dally if she wants to get to the zoo. Meanwhile, the cloud that looks like a cute white elephant builds up into a dark grey herd of elephants, and the book ends with the mom drawing the curtain closed: it's too late to go, the rain is starting and the zoo is about to close. The lesson is simply, You see what happens when you think you have all the time in the world? But the lesson did nothing to soothe the terror.

When she looked at the American girl, she saw skittishness, pain, and a stubborn desire for connection. She let herself imagine a humble house in a Midwest American suburb, filled with the ethic of hard work and good grades; then sudden ill-ness in the family, a poor prognosis, and finally, the painful attempt to waste no time and take one last, iconic trip as a family — Paris.

She thinks of her family house in Croatia, the house her parents fixed slowly and painfully, stopping every time the money ran out. It ran out often, because the war forced them into early retirement, and because her mom wanted not only to patch things up, but to make things better — more expen-sive tile, the latest blinds. By the time they were done, they seemed jaded and jagged from the effort. But the house, indeed, was beautiful. So much so that it tempted Mira to imagine herself living there. The stone tile in the yard where the wicker furniture was set up, and that curving path — which the workers had to redo about three times until her mother was satisfied — that led to the huge rose patch. The guest bedroom window opened up to it. Even that bedroom had a series of small original paintings of wheat fields hung gallery-style on the wall — somewhat generic, but still pleasing, a gift from some regular hotel guest.

After Dad's funeral, a sweaty day, early in August, they had lined up spare tables in the yard and served smoked meat and cheese and cakes and mineral water and juice and beer. At that table, in response to someone saying kindly, "You've made a home to be proud of," her mother, about to bite into a coconut chocolate square, said, "My home is with my daughters." She said it with the flatness of a wooden plank, but still, it was confirmation of affinity. Mira and her sister looked at each other like two people who have simultaneously realized the tide has changed and they better watch what happens next.

But nothing happened until this mini-stroke, this sinister warning. Mira thought, some people, maliciously, love this kind of story: bad things happening when you might expect a rest, might expect some shade after a day spent toiling under a fickle sun. All of them but Dad are still under the sun. How should one toil to earn one's rest?

Now Mira comes inside from the balcony, arms and legs seared by cold. She peeks in on the pigeon. It seems alert, picking at the crust she has broken into small pieces, and she wonders, is it satisfied? You're just convalescing, little guy, she tells it, you won't stay inside this box forever.

She walks over to her suitcase to find some clothes, and as she's pushing aside her blouses and pants, her phone keeps beeping notifications. So she chucks it across the room. She should do that more often — the thing never breaks anyway. But the pigeon goes into an anxious shuffle and flutter when the phone hits the ground near its box. It's alright, it's alright, she calls out to it.

She goes down for breakfast. In the dining room she is alone. No Merima. No Americans. It's too bad — she misses all of them. An unfamiliar woman brings her a breakfast tray, and she drinks the whole pot of coffee, one cup after another, with quick warming gulps.

She gets out and walks on the large boulevard rather than the quieter streets where she and Bernard started out on their bike ride on the first day. Not many people around. A couple of thug-like teenagers jostling each other as they wait to cross the road: what is with those oversized track suits, that slouching, yet tense, posture? And why are they even up this early?

She passes baffling sandwich shop displays: row upon row of long buns, jammed in like sweating sausages, the lettuce already wilting and the meat curling at the edges where it peeks out. She's seen these everywhere, and they're always full: what on earth for? Who buys them? Like the keychains of the Eiffel Tower, reproductions without purpose or end. How long do they sit under that glass? Do they throw out the whole batch of them and make another hundred to throw out the next day?

The air loses some of its morning coolness and she can already sense the heat of the day. She veers off the boulevard and heads roughly south, away from the river; she's not brought her purse and has neither wallet nor guidebook nor phone. Her sense of direction is tentative, at best. She walks into a park — endless parks in this city — and sits down on one of the benches lining the gravel path. She and an elderly, kerchiefed woman in a beige raincoat, walking a grey and white mutt on a leash, are the only people there. Mira looks at the ground: pebbles at her feet, fine gradations of greyness. Without looking up she can see the small dog sniffing a bench, a rosebush, the low iron fence. The elderly woman's shoes are the kind of orthopedic, wedge-heel shoes that nurses used to wear. How should one toil to earn one's rest? *When our lives were surely past noon.* "I'm learning to cook," Mirko had said in his letter, "and I never thought I'd care so much about the perfect doneness of an omelette." And she'd never replied.

After a while there is another pair of feet, the fringe of a skirt. Mira looks up — a young woman has sat down on another bench, holding something in cupped hands. She extends her legs wide and releases whatever it is into the crotch part of her long green skirt. It seems to be a pile of small rocks. This woman also has the small, heart-shaped face reminiscent of Aisha's. Who'd have thought there'd be a legion of Aisha-lookalikes, turning up all over Paris?

Or is it actually the same woman, the one from Champs-Élysées, the one Bernard so audaciously talked to in Montmartre? That same small build, frizzy hair, flowing skirt?

The woman starts throwing the rocks, lightly, onto the path in front of her. She takes aim and tries to hit those rocks already on the ground: she lobs gently, misses, then tries to half-throw, half-roll. And so on. Like bocce ball. Though her back is slouched, her attempts are measured and earnest. When she runs out of rocks, she gets up to collect them — skirt tucked between knees, frizzy bun unravelling on her neck — and resumes her game. Mira finds it easy to stare from behind sunglasses, pretending to look into the middle distance at the manicured trees.

Then two men walk across fenced-off grass and come up behind the bench. They speak loudly to this young woman, who doesn't look at them, merely yells something back and throws more rocks. One man jostles her shoulder as if to push her off. The other one laughs. Then the first one pushes her harder. The woman with the mutt walks calmly down a path leading out of the park, tugging just gently on the dog's leash. Mira cannot tell how much the young woman on the bench is afraid of the men. Her face does not change much, until she does stand up. Then there is hard fury in it, visible even from a distance.

But the standing up is concession, after all, defeat; she's got up to join them. When one of the men swats the back of her head lightly, she strikes out at him, and he, in an exaggerated way, almost as if he were dancing, moves his upper body away from her hand, and laughs anew. They cannot stop laughing, these two. The young woman looks as if she hasn't a laugh in any of her bones.

Maybe that is not true. Maybe it is just how things look right now. She must have laughed, sometime, in joy rather than jest or contempt.

"This is the world," Mira says to herself. "Through random selection, some people are free and some are not."

The pebbles at her feet click when she runs her foot over them. Free.

There's no sense to it, Merima had said, just randomness and coincidence. Yet there she was, with her own perfect boy — her two perfect boys.

She gets up from the bench and ends up following the woman and men from a great distance. It's not a completely conscious decision until she is out of the park and sees them far ahead of her on the street. They are going farther south, perhaps — that's about all she can glean from the sun's position. It is not, in any case, a part of Paris she has walked through before. The three walk briskly, but here and there stop for one of the men to light a cigarette. Mira tries to look like she is minding her own business. The buildings here look largely residential, with shops on the ground, cars and motorbikes parked at an angle in front of them. When they turn right, she makes the same turn; when they go left, she goes left too. They pass one landmark Mira has heard of, the Montparnasse cemetery.

After that, though she reads the street names, they offer no clues — she recognizes nothing.

She sees them enter what looks like a small grocery, and after a few minutes only two of them come out, one of the men and the woman, the woman carrying a small bag. Mira approaches the shop and before she knows why she's doing it, she walks in. It is the size of a bathroom. In the tiny square of space behind the counter, below uneven, crammed shelves, sits a man with earbuds in his ears, talking hands-free to someone through a cell phone. His beard reaches mid-chest, a beard so healthy it looks unreal. The shelves are packed with biscuits, bread, dried fruit, coffee, tea, dish detergent, tampons; if you weren't choosy, you could buy everything here. There is no sign of the other man. She buys, stupidly, two bananas from the bunch by the cash register, with a single euro she finds in her pants pocket, and walks out.

She keeps going in the same direction as the woman and the man, when they left the store moments ago. When she spots a garbage can, she drops the two bananas into it. The blue street sign says Rue de Gergovie. That was the street name in the address she found under Mirko's last name in the directory, wasn't it? She keeps going and soon, among the parked cars and the thin trees, she glimpses the young woman's long green skirt. But now the other man seems gone too, and instead of him with her is a child, a little boy.

If she had brought her phone, she would try to connect to a map to see where she is. Nothing is frightening here, the street ordinary, a few people going about their weekday, late-morning business, but the transformations of the group have unsettled her. She knows that if you're going to follow, you've got to be willing to end up somewhere unpredictable: you've got be willing to look at a place you don't recognize. Yet she also knows that if she comes within sight of an ugly place — although there is no trace of it yet — some tent encampment with mangy hungry dogs and clothes drying on stacked bricks, a place with the heady smell of the unfamiliar or perhaps the frighteningly familiar, she will stop and not look further.

She's been walking, she guesses, more than an hour — like a teenager without her phone, she doesn't even know the time — and she wonders if the woman has somewhere to get to, or will keep strolling in this undefined way, making her companions disappear or shape-shift. She and the boy hold hands, swing their arms, cross streets without waiting for green lights.

When the boy points left, they turn a corner. But when Mira does the same, they are gone. She looks keenly down the length of the street. She looks left and right cautiously, uneasy about perhaps having been spotted. Uneasy that things can just disappear.

She should have figured. Every chase ends that way. Still, it unreasonably disappoints her.

She notices that up the street is a church, angular and pale brown: perhaps they've gone inside. She walks up to it, then turns the corner, looking for the door. There is a recessed side door, and in the vestibule two elderly people have set up blankets and cardboard boxes, and they huddle there in over-sized raincoats and white sneakers. Next to them, green skirt spread like an indulgence around her, is the young woman, cradling the boy in her lap.

And crouching with his back to Mira, holding a to-go cup with two hands, a man she recognizes despite not seeing his face.

She doesn't move. The old couple has noticed her by now, but they, perhaps because they are themselves so often unseen, look past her, through her, into the street, of which she is one unexceptional part.

The man is soft-looking, wearing a beige shirt and beige slacks, his hair gone to a thin, messy shag, combed down but still unruly, white and light brown: a soft, beige man. From the back, he could have been anyone — an office worker, a week-end cyclist, a Parisian, a Tunisian, a Croatian, an urban middle-aged professional at home in late-capitalist western society.

He is nodding at the little boy, then patting the boy's cheek, and then he's up. When he notices Mira, waves of shock, then adjustment, then again disbelief, pass clearly over his face.

In their youngest youth before the war, he had been gre-garious. It is the English word that comes to her as the fitting one. A loud, generous, funny young man. Brimming. The vig-our of him. Now he looks deflated, thinned out; his button-up shirt hangs loose and askew. But still, he exclaims her name with wonder.

"Mira! How did you appear here?"

BERNARD IS ALONE, at the same café on the Champs-Élysées where he sat with Mira on their first day. Just two days earlier, and yet a long time ago. Alice is spending the day with her parents — it's their last day in Paris, too, so they're making a day trip to Versailles. She rushed to meet them before breakfast ended. He even considered asking to join them, but stopped short. Would that have been a boundary issue? His counselor talked a lot about boundaries. He thought it might be and got too shy. Afterwards, he looked for Mira, but she wasn't in her room. He tried again in a little while, but nothing. This was a little baffling. Where would she have gone? And she wasn't answering her phone. Was she avoiding him because of the Alice thing? It's really too bad she had to head into the shower right at that moment. But then again, she's not his mom, so she shouldn't get mad at him for that, should she?

She's always been so nice to him, and especially when he was a little kid.

He'd intended to retrace his and Aisha's trip into the Marais. To find the tiny falafel restaurant where a mouse ran past their table, and when one of a group of Italians seated nearby jumped up, incensed, the waitress, surely enjoying herself, said, "You're afraid of a little mouse? This is Paris, it's full of mice!" Before noon tomorrow he and Mira will be on the subway taking them out to Charles de Gaulle, which means he's running out of time for his task of retracing his and Aisha's steps in Paris. He had an itinerary! But he strayed from it already on the first night when Mahue took him to her room. And now, instead of the Marais, he's ended up here, with a beer and a strange lukewarm quiche. Maybe when he finds Mira, they could go to the Marais together in the afternoon. There was still today, all of today, after all.

Talking to that girl in Montparnasse yesterday, Janina, in that strange dip — hole? — in the ground was odd and exhilarating, like going through a secret door behind which was a secret club.

He wandered back to the metro, after following her directions for getting back the way they came. Everything he saw seemed enlivened: a vast, extraordinary network of signs, a jungle of insights, every person a possibility of new knowledge. It maybe was or wasn't uncanny that her questions, her subtle silliness even, had the very tenor and tone of Aisha. Intelligence without pretense. If only they could go for a drink or something — really talk. There is so much he'd like to know.

All the way back to the hotel he continued an imaginary conversation with her. Then the imaginary conversation with her somehow turned into a conversation with Aisha — at first,

Aisha was in the audience, a curious third, then he was address-
ing her, reporting to her what seemed most interesting about
Janina.

It was a muddle, in short.

Now he is alone, his beer is nearly finished, and he's abandoned his quiche long ago. It sits on the plate like a lump of
pudding sprinkled with parsley.

So he's grateful when a text buzzes. *I found this link*, it says,
for an herb they use in Nepal for blood clots to prevent strokes.
Apparently available in Europe, also? Silly, but, you know, placebo
effects? Well. Aisha may have her veterinarian, is living with
him, even, but she still checks on Bernard and worries about
his grandmother. But that's always been Aisha — that kind of
goodness. At least he's always thought of that as goodness.

And yet, despite talking to her in his mind so much, he
can't write back. For the first time that he can remember, he's
not answered her texts for more than a day, for several days.
Somehow, it just won't do to have a faux-light exchange about
weird herbs. Do better, he wants to yell, that won't do! You owe
me more than that! But that's the rub — she owes him precisely
nothing and would be well within her rights to never say or
write a single word to him again. And what does he owe her?

He pays the bill and walks down the Champs-Élysées, away
from the Grand Arch. His phone dings again, and he stops in
the shade to check it. Maybe it would be Mira, finally — he's
worried, it being past noon already. No, it's spam mail, delete.
Why won't she even text him?

Two guys stop on the sidewalk, not far from where he's standing, and one points at him. Bernard looks behind him — no one there. He returns to his phone, but they start talking quickly, pointing with their chins in his direction, arguing. They are youngish, thin men, wearing fake-distressed jeans and dirty white runners; one unshaven in a scruffy, messy way, the other with deliberate thin lines flanking his jaw. Is it really him they're looking at? Their theatrics baffle and annoy him. He's not afraid — hard to be afraid when it's morning, and you're on an open, ordinary, sunny street. But it does seem a confirmation of something being wrong about this whole day. He begins to walk, briskly.

In that same moment, both men rush toward him. They yell at him in quick foreign words, their tone aggrieved and accusing. One is shaking his finger, scolding! Bernard is at first embarrassed — what a scene he is suddenly in the centre of! — and then realizes that there's been a misunderstanding: they think he's someone else. Or, he's offended them, unknowingly, somehow — he tries to picture what he was doing moments before, walking away from the café, simply stopping to check his phone.

One man pushes him on the chest, hard enough that he stumbles backwards and hits his back against a tree, and then the other quickly slaps him on the side of his head so that his ear rings; Bernard pushes back, with both arms, then remembers to form a fist, and goes for the neck — one of their necks — as hard as he can. Everything is cursing and the smell of sour sweat and muskiness and an alcoholic tang of cologne. He swings again, but suddenly his eye and the whole half of his face explode with tearing, terrifying pain. He doesn't know what he's doing, only that his arms are up over his throbbing head, and a car is honking insistently. He's lost his balance in curling up — or have they tripped him, tangled his legs? — and he feels a blunt kick to his backside — Jesus, will it go on, and his eye, his eye — and then they are running, he hopes they are running; the honking stops, and he is suddenly aware of the smell of grass and steps approaching him.

"JUST GO ON, feel free," Mirko says, and so she enters a dim, cool place, with him behind her, he closing the door gently, setting his keys on a hook, unlacing his shoes, patiently doing all he must do on any day he enters his home. She sees him drop his watch onto a small plate that sits on a narrow chest of drawers.

"Feel free," he says again, to propel her through the short hallway into the next room, which turns out to be the kitchen. There is a small table for four in the middle, sink and stove and fridge against the back wall, a carton of milk and a couple of dried-up peach pits on the counter between sink and stove. It's the configuration of a rural kitchen, the kitchens of their grandparents. The window seems oddly placed on the left wall. Dark blue curtain. She thinks the window must look onto the street they came in from, but the room feels insular, removed.

"You want to drink something? Lemonade?"

I make it myself, she wants him to say. Somehow I enjoy doing it. Isn't it funny the things we do now?

"Yes."

He opens the fridge, brings out a pitcher, takes down two tall, narrow glasses from a cupboard.

She has forgotten to take off her shoes.

The floor is linoleum, with a pattern of square grey tiles.

Stop observing the room. The room could be anything. The thing is, she's just unprepared.

Mirko has his back to her, pouring lemonade. The glasses start to fog from the coldness of the drink.

One time they were so drunk together that they started rolling spontaneously from the top of a hill all the way down into a creek, laughing helplessly, yelping when they got closer to the water. Mirko's shirt had rolled up, and she remembers the gleaming white of his soft round stomach, the tiny brown nipples, and a mole like a tiny pebble beneath one of them. It's poking me, he'd yelled, pull down my shirt! But that was as impossible as their not rolling into the creek. You could not tell in that state what was willed and what was the energy of the world propelling you. They laughed even as they stood up unsteadily in the muddy water, their shoes and clothes half-soaked.

All that time they were not lovers. How stupid to not have been.

Several years later, after being sparsely in touch during the whole war, he wrote her the letter that arrived at her sister's Canadian address, the letter she kept but never answered. He wrote it from a bee farm where a dozen men with PTSD learned to tend bees; they had lodging in small private cabins, and food in a communal kitchen in the middle of the property. In the letter, he listed the food that arrived on small trucks and they had to put away every Tuesday: fresh cheese from a nearby sheep farm, eggs and whole hens, potatoes and carrots and tomatoes and mushrooms, apples and rice and butter. Bread came every day. Honey, of course, that was breakfast. They cooked chicken paprikash, mushroom risotto, ate cold platters of bread and cheese, spread honey on bread and fruit and even put it in their coffee. He said all this in the letter. He said, I cannot get over it: I am obsessed with the food.

He wrote that in the prisoners' camp they'd tortured him with electricity. They sit you down and tell you to pull down your pants and they attach a prod to your balls. They start taunting you with things they want you to say — that you hate them, or that you've murdered their mothers. When you don't say it they zap, and when you do say it, they zap. I don't need to explain what this feels like, he wrote. The worst is looking around the room, because you realize how much you are where you are and nowhere else.

It is easier to tell stories in general terms, harder to relive the details, he wrote. Before we were brought to the camp, they'd shut us into this warehouse, more than a hundred of us, a warehouse like any other, with a tall ceiling, small windows high up. It was dark, after midnight. Men sat on the floor hugging their knees. One held his head in his hands so you couldn't see his face, just blood dripping between his shaking fingers. He wore a black leather jacket. A candle was lit in front of him — I don't know where the candle had come from, whether he'd carried it in his jacket pocket, along with matches and a knife perhaps, following his survival training — and he was reciting verses from a small Bible that lay opened next to the candle. I couldn't tell, Mirko wrote, if he was actually reading from behind his hands as they covered his face, but then the candle tipped over, someone stomped on it to extinguish it, and then there was just the sound of his voice reciting, I suppose, from memory, in the darkness.

Later, in the camp, nights were often interrupted by men being taken away. Some were gone for hours and then thrown in moaning and remained on the floor calling out for their mothers. You must hear this to understand, where it grips you — not even in the pit of the stomach, but the loins. It's not only the pain of the moment, which is great, but the knowledge that some of these men would not be good for anything anymore — not for being lovers or fathers or friends. Occasionally there was a gunshot after someone was led out. I was trying to remember everybody because I thought there would be a day when someone would call on us for these names.

He wrote all this in a letter precisely to her. Her name and her sister's address, the only one he had. On the back of the envelope the name of the mountain road where the bee farm stood.

She had wanted so much to hear something from him. To be in his confidence, to be reassured he was alright.

To know he was still himself. But he sounded like someone else — or like some new, unsettling manifestation of himself.

Although she didn't answer the letter, she did find him at the farm on her first brief trip back home. He was still there: you could stay for as long as two years, and then you had to clear room for others.

They sat on the bed in his cabin. A narrow and hard bed, like the beds of her student residence. She was looking for clues in the room, and she had some — a full ashtray, a tiny coil-bound notepad, open to a page filled with writing, bulging, it seemed, from the force of the handwriting on its tiny pages. A pillow on the floor, next to the small desk made of unfinished pine.

But she must not have interpreted the clues well enough, or at all. What she said to him was, "What you went through was horrible. But if I have learned anything through all this shit, it's that you must put the past into the past. After I visited Danijela in that psychiatric ward, I put all our letters and notes and pictures and all the crap we ever gave each other in a box, and took the box to the trash. It was so liberating. If you like, we could, together, burn this letter you've written to me. You've got it all out in there, right? And now it's done. You don't have to live with it anymore."

Did she really believe it was that easy to free yourself? She even packed a lighter and a can in her backpack, and took them out, ready. "You know the woods around here," she said. "We could go somewhere secluded, burn it, then put out the fire, and it will be done once and for all."

He looked perplexed — or so she interprets it now, that he was perplexed, and maybe also in despair. He told her just to put all that away and to walk with him through the grounds.

They did. She was impatient, waiting for him to return to the subject of the letter. But he was simply, she thought, dazed.

After the walk, he kept her for their evening meal, evening being five p.m. on their schedule. As the meal went on, he looked more and more distant and became more and more clumsy. He pushed squares of cheese at her to try and they tumbled onto the floor. He ignored the mess near their feet, and she was too self-conscious to bend down and try to retrieve the pieces. He spoke to her about the mushrooms having been picked by a man who'd picked mushrooms here for decades. But he left this and other thoughts unfinished.

Because he can't let go of the past, she had thought. Instead he is decoying with cheese and apples and cured ham. The foolishness, she had thought. Only years later did she think of herself as the fool.

She stayed after dinner; they were alone in his cabin again, but they did not make love then either. She tried to reminisce with him, as she had with Danijela: to find happy memories that would remind them both of who they were. It must not have been the right thing to do, because he only smoked more the more she talked. And by the time she was leaving, his distance gave way to something hard and watchful. He made a derisive joke about her backpack.

"You came here looking like you're ready to hike the mountain," he said.

It hurt her. He hadn't been that way before. But then again, she thought, we've all been smashed up, and some much more than others. Our moods are not what they used to be. We change, with more suddenness, quickness, and maliciousness than before. She must've known, too, that happy memories could not lead them back to those other, younger people.

"Thank you for dinner," she said. "I'll never forget those mushrooms. They were really spectacular."

If he would not burn the letter, there was no sense in her burning it, and it stayed among her other postcards and photographs, the random ones she hadn't thrown away. Because in fact the desire to trash things left her very quickly after her initial vigour, and she didn't bother with sorting, either.

Next time she made it back home to visit her parents, she didn't look him up. She was there with David, for the first time, and their timelines for different visits, the places she needed to show him, were taut and inflexible. It was perhaps the tensest vacation they ever had. But her dad reminded her of Mirko one afternoon, when he said, "You see, for instance, the government has money to buy itself a hundred brand new Audis with leather seats but doesn't have money for a program like that bee farm for men with mental difficulties—that syndrome—"

He was talking about the Croatian government, of course. She was wearing her hair in sloppy ponytails then, and she remembers how she'd yanked on the elastic, for no reason, and the hot pain of many tiny hairs being pulled shot through her head. David sat next to her in her parents' living room, twirling cherries in a small glass of her mother's cherry brandy. They were at the beginning of their joyful, heartbreaking marriage. Mirko would have been out of the program by then, anyway. She didn't know where he was and chose not to ask her parents if they did.

Later that day, and intermittently over the years, without apparent cause, she would think of something she had eaten at the farm. The spoonful of honey she was given to try as soon as she arrived. Rolls of ham, soft and deeply pink-red, like petals. The creamy risotto she had taken seconds of, with soft bits of bacon fat and brown mushroom flecks.

Now, there is lemonade. Nicely done, barely sweet, fresh. He must make it himself.

His face looks calm, a face that has settled into a shape — smile lines, forehead grooves.

"The city's been deporting Romas. At one point they were giving two hundred euros to anyone willing to go back where they came from — mostly they've come from Rumania or Bulgaria — if they promised they would not return to France. That older couple took the money last year and went back. But things were just as bad as always, and they did return. So now — they're not supposed to be here, and they don't have the money to go anywhere else."

"I saw that young woman in the park and followed her."

"Klementina. We play checkers together. The church has charity dinners sometimes, so I cook, serve soup, eat with those who come around. That's one thing I can do, cook."

She senses stubbornness, defensiveness, and understands that she is a representative of a world, the world of back home, that has judged him a failure. Or — the world that he's judged a failure.

"What are you doing here? Do you have someone in Paris?"

"I'm here with my nephew. We're going home in a few days. No, tomorrow actually. My mom had a stroke, or a mini-stroke, I guess — I wrote it in that note, which I don't know if you got — anyway, we just stopped here because my nephew thought it's a good chance to spend a few days in Paris."

He doesn't pause or look away at the mention of her note, gives no sign of notice.

"How old is he?"

"Twenty-three. How old is Ante now?" She was thinking of the red-headed boy she had doubled on her bike so many years ago.

"Twenty-eight. You should see him. He's a giant. Has two kids, twins."

"Jesus. Well, of course." They would not ask each other about children, husbands, wives. "I'm sorry," she says. "I'm embarrassed to be here."

His face looks slightly pained. He looks away from her toward the blue curtain.

I've not asked you here.

Is it my job to make you feel better?

He may as well have said those aloud, they seem so obvious.

She is blushing, a rare thing, no helping it.

"I'm ashamed of the things I've said, the ways I've acted."

Foolish, to persist. Who isn't?

"I'm surprised you've looked me up after this many years. Your mother, father, sister, where are they?"

"Dad died. Two years ago. It was a shock."

She sees how things are now — how he lets only some reactions register on his face and parses out his words carefully.

"I'm sorry. I liked him, you know."

She knows everyone had liked her dad, but it still hurts equally each time someone says so.

"Well. I want to show you something I got from him."

He leaves down another hallway, not the one they came in through, and returns with a wooden box that he sets down on the table. Then he opens a cupboard to bring out a bag of cookies, vanilla cream wafers, which he shakes out onto a plain white plate.

"I'm sorry I don't have much to offer here right now. I've been away for a little while. I have thought of you over the years." He speaks more quickly now and his hands fidget on the table after he's set the plate on it.

She thinks of the word *generation*. We are of a generation. What has our generation done in the world?

"I don't keep much, but I've kept this."

The box he's brought is the kind their grandfathers kept their rolling tobacco in. He lifts the lid and takes out a palm-sized transistor radio the shape and colour of a ladybug, a cheap novelty item from the '70s.

"Your dad gave me this. It was in the early years after the war. I don't know where you were, but I'd come to your folks' house — they were putting in new hardwood. There were boxes of things he was going through, and I picked this up, for no reason. He'd bought a pair of these for you girls, he said, but one had got lost, and this one survived. He said I should take it as a memento from him, and one day when he's under the earth I'll remember him. So I took it. I liked him, you know."

Foolish never to have made love. Nothing should ever be saved for later. But even as she thinks it, she doesn't know if she believes it.

"The box was my father's," he continues. "I like to keep that generation of men together. They were born to fathers and mothers who carried the other war in them, who themselves were born into war, or out of it. They had that whole legacy, the false categories of fascism and freedom. Maybe the categories aren't false but what history places inside them. Worn stories, to them, uninteresting, but even tired stories get under our skin. They did some good. Some of them lived with integrity in a corrupt system."

"And look at us."

But that seems cruel, to hold them up, to hold him up, after all his suffering.

"The thing that has bothered me for many years, has been that the men who did the groundwork evil of this war have been the stupidest, the cruelest, the most maladapted among us. Losers. People who in high school thought it was funny to piss on teachers' cars. People you wouldn't go for a beer with. Then you're in a room with those same losers and they have the power to kill you or ruin your life. But this is what history is."

"Dad said once that serving in the army taught him a good lesson: that life is about accepting any fool in the right uniform can make you do things you don't want to do."

"But then," he continued, "I thought later, what does my idea imply? That men who aren't losers doing evil is better? That having the brains beaten out of you by men who are smarter and more sophisticated than you would be better?" He taps his palm lightly on the table. "I'm sorry. I'm sorry. These are not things we need to talk about."

In some part of the apartment a door opens and is carefully shut. Mirko doesn't turn his head. She does, and sees a woman materialize from the darkness of the hallway, moving slowly on crutches, the kind of crutches that hold each arm below the elbow. Her thin legs twist inward at the knees, and her grey-brown hair is combed backwards, several sections of it separating with wetness, or grease.

She is eerily thin, with thick veins weaving around stubborn muscle; her face is all eyes, hollowed out cheeks, and skin drooping in small folds around the eyes and mouth and chin.

"Bonjour," she says, in a raspy voice, when she is already past them and reaching for a cup in the cupboard, having freed her left hand of the crutch. She uses the same hand to pour lemonade from the pitcher on the counter.

Mira can imagine words used to describe such women, women ill and thin and hollowed out-looking, dismissed with one nasty word. She thinks, anything can be reduced to meaninglessness, a hollow category, merely out of habit. The nasty words appeared unbidden, both hers and not. The woman is possibly young enough to be Mirko's wife — a home with a wife in it, after all.

The woman leans her crutches against the counter and sits down slowly at the table. Mirko moves her glass of lemonade from the counter to the table in front of her.

He and she speak to each other, quickly, in French. "This is Larissa," he says, switching now to English.

"You speak English?" Larissa says then, looking at Mira directly for the first time.

"I live in Canada."

"And how do you like Paris?" The inflection of the question and the way the woman's mouth twists at the end of it infuse it with such contempt that Mira is not sure if she is meant to answer, or how; and is it contempt for her, or for the city?

"I like it quite a lot. I've never been before."

"You haven't been to the suburbs, either, I imagine," Larissa says. "You should. Everyone should go."

"I've already met one person who told me immigrants are ruining the city. I suppose the tourists aren't helping either."

Larissa blinks, as if blinking away a petty obstacle, an irrelevant distraction.

"You misunderstand me," Larissa says. "I'm talking about the terrible way people are made to live — this —" Instead of finishing the sentence, she waves her hand as if shooing a fly — as if the conclusion is clear, or, perhaps, useless to explain to this audience.

"Are you in pain today?" Mirko says, quietly.

She waves that away too.

Was he handling her, as you would a child, a not-fully-rational person?

"There is all kinds of vice here!" She turns pointedly to Mira now, seeking her audience, her pitch rising. "And it's the vice of the haves!"

Mirko holds a kitchen towel in his fist and Mira notices his fist get tighter.

"Larissa thinks there will be more riots," Mirko says, his voice now teasing, almost mocking. "Sometimes I think she wishes for them. Do you?"

"There is desperation among those people. Of course there is! I could provide you with statistics, and they would shock you. Shock you!"

"Settle down," Mirko says, and releases the kitchen towel so it sits crumpled innocently next to his hand. His voice is a slice of cold ham slapped down on a cold plate.

The tone startles Mira, the way a cool current in a warm sea will startle you. And it changes, very slightly, Larissa's posture. She runs her hand over her hair, smoothing it down. Mira can see it is wet hair, combed after a bath; she smells some cheap and gentle shampoo, some chamomile scent from a bottom shelf.

Mira takes measured sips of her lemonade. Everyone looks away from everyone else.

Then Larissa says, her pitch now ordinary and conversational, "Oui, it is as it is. Some pain."

Mirko smooths out the towel under his hand. Larissa turns to Mira and continues, "I have all kinds of problems. Legs, liver, bones." She laughs. "Head!" She raises her lemonade glass. "To Paris the great!" Her laugh is raspy but sympathetic, earnest.

Mira smiles, makes a slight gesture of a toast, and drains her glass.

"It is almost time for my physio. Would you take me today? It will be quicker than —"

She is speaking English but Mirko answers in French, something quick and affirmative. And to Mira, in Croatian now, he says, "Why don't you come with us? I can drop you off afterwards, wherever you need to go."

He begins to clear the glasses, and Larissa smooths her hair again.

Mira is stuck for a long moment, and finally she says, "It's not necessary. I can walk."

"Don't be silly. We can talk more in the car. Where are you staying?"

"I don't know." Really, she does, of course, know the name of the hotel.

"I'm going to change my shirt," Larissa says. She uses both arms on the unsteady table to prop herself up, rocking the plate of wafers so that a few slide from the plate onto the table. It is a slow half minute during which she takes the crutches Mirko passes her and leaves the kitchen, moving into the depth of the hallway she came out of.

"You don't know where you're staying," Mirko says, with his back to Mira, arranging glasses in the sink. "I might have expected that."

He then opens the cupboard door beneath the sink, takes the plate of wafers, ignoring the ones fallen onto the table, and slides them all cleanly into the garbage.

After the door of the cabinet slams, he is gone, within a moment, down the same hallway. Mira is still sitting — she has hardly moved. Everything seems exceptionally still.

In a corner of the counter, where earlier she noticed only a few dried-out peach pits, instead of them she now sees a robust-looking pomegranate. A pomegranate!

That is what she would like to eat, not those pale crumbly wafers. Still, he shouldn't have dumped them in the garbage.

I might have expected that.

And you couldn't go looking through someone's drawers for a suitable knife and start cutting up a pomegranate, spilling its red juice, right on their off-white counter.

The next day, she and Bernard would fly to Zagreb. Maybe she could write Mirko a letter? A long email explaining why she couldn't stay and accept a ride, though she had wanted so much to see him, had been granted an extraordinary coincidence?

Has she also planned many letters to David, and begun some, and sent none? Is that the kind of person she was? Yes. So the letter thing may not be reliable. Maybe, in this situation, the act of attempting letters was like trying to capture in words a dream after the fact of dreaming — at best something partial and convoluted and inadequate.

She stands up. Why is this place so dark? It's not a basement, for goodness' sake. She wonders whether this is the ordinary state of things here, or she has stumbled into some kind of an unraveling. She walks over to the window and moves aside the curtain, only to find that she is about waist-level with the pavement outside: one of those half-sunk ground floors. Somehow she had not noticed the descent.

She hears his steps behind her and turns.

"I hadn't noticed the slope when we came in."

"No one does."

"I don't know which way you would drive from here to my hotel," she says, "but I can go with you to the physio — wherever you're going — and you can drop me afterward, if you like."

THEY DRIVE THROUGH what seems like half of Paris and leave Larissa in a bright clinic waiting room. Then they drive some more, stop at a Tabak, park, and walk to a garden, where they stand and smoke cigarettes by a stone sculpture of an anonymous woman.

They judge it a woman by the hair in a bun and small breasts, but it is a heavy-limbed, wide-shouldered, square-jawed woman, sitting on her haunches on a rectangular platform. A woman boxy in the way of something pressing down on her, like in the cartoons where the anvil flattens the characters — as if something has pushed her closer to the ground and nearly flattened her.

Mira hasn't smoked a cigarette in years, yet it doesn't nauseate her at all. Mirko doesn't smoke either, anymore, but it is one thing they used to do together and that seems fitting for this moment.

"I've never understood how they communicate all that with stone. With dead matter." Mirko leans his palm against the woman's shoulder, squeezing a cigarette between the knuckles of his other hand. There is in fact already a litter of cigarette butts around the stone, and one of the woman's knees looks worn in, as if people regularly use it for sitting on. Both of them lean every which way, rest their palms on her, then their elbows and their backs. They roll the soles of their shoes over her hips.

"Larissa used to be different," he says. "She's helped me a lot. She used to practice reiki. Do you know what reiki is? And acupuncture. She did a lot of work on me. What was between us wasn't romantic, you understand. But she has done a lot for me."

Mira has a vague sense that he isn't wholly telling the truth. That he is perhaps finding a fine point of balance between loyalty and the need for distance. His male ego's need for distance?

"She lives with you?"

"It's a temporary solution. Probably. But it suits me fine. I'm happy to help her. She's a good person when she's not in too much pain."

Waiting at red lights, Mirko massaged his neck with relentless intensity, pushed all his four fingers into the back of it again and again, like some essential self-therapy. But when the light changed, he would brush his hand upward through his hair, casually, then put both hands back on the steering wheel, appearing patient in the tight squeeze turns and sudden stops.

Blessed are the poor in spirit, the patient in traffic, the mourners, the reluctant smokers.

Then he says, "It never occurred to me back then that you might not write back, just as it wouldn't have occurred to me to write that stuff to anyone but you. I wrote it as if I were speaking to you, having the sickest conversation of my life. I'd get light-headed. My right arm would grow numb. I left the letter for weeks at a time. I drank. There were long nights by the toilet bowl, my own dried-up urine leaving a stain on my cheek. It's disgusting, I'm sorry, but that's how it was. But I made myself put the papers in an envelope, copy the address I had, and go to the post office. Maybe you remember I didn't even sign off properly — I wrote Tvoj Mirko underneath an unfinished sentence."

The sun burns her face as she looks at him saying it.

"I'd be lying if I said I did it only for my own relief. It looks that way — as if I needed an imaginary listener, a blank humanity. Maybe in person I'd never have spoken aloud. But still. I really did wait for you to say something. In a letter, or a phone call. I know it would have been a short one, because the call rates were through the roof then. I waited for a few weeks, because it took that long for a letter to travel. Then a few months. You were choosing your words, I thought, and you had a lot to say."

He smiles — deliberately, perhaps, to help her out.

"I guess I did say something, but too late, and the wrong thing."

That day with him at the farm has pinged around her brain for many years, each ping a little painful wham. The cornbread they had eaten in the hills, crumbly but elastic. Its revision, the improved day, also pinged about: she showed up with open hands, carried no matches in her backpack, they sat on a tree stump smelling the pine trees, they parted with affection, broken but loyal. He maybe even sent her home with a backpack of cornbread and honey, sharing the plenty.

"I'm sorry," she says. "I wish I had done differently. At some point I started to live inside the wish as if inside a second skin, a second life."

In another revision that floats about her mind, she and David take their coffee on a balcony that looks out to the Barents Sea in the distance. That coffee would be excellent, like the muesli and the public transportation. But they wouldn't care for swimming in the Barents Sea too much. They'd be flying to the Adriatic every chance they had. In that way, by a long circuitous route, David would maybe have brought her home.

Blessed are the guilty, the regretters, the revisers, the would-have-beeners, the stubborn wishful-thinkers, the repentant and self-flagellating perfectionists, the unforgiven, the ones come too late to the zoo.

She laughs, digs her toes into the gravel. The foolishness.

Mirko says, "Oh, I don't know that it would've changed anything. It's just something I wished for. You can't be sure what it looks like to get what you think you want, anyway."

"I'm sorry."

"We were just babies, and full of rage."

"I suppose."

Then he says, "I don't know what to do with all that stuff either, the people we used to be. They don't burn well."

She and Mirko lean for a long time; they smoke all the cigarettes, and the sun beats down on their uncovered heads and their badly parted hair. They squint and get dry-mouthed. They remember other sunned afternoons and wish for some of the rains from the east that, as Mirko tells her — as Ljilja told her too, she remembers now — are soaking their former homes. Then Larissa phones and tells them the time: the time is for going back, even if going back can't be called going home.

Of course, they would not make love now either, wouldn't return to his half-sunk apartment and spend the evening reminiscing and lolling about and rearranging their lives for each other. She feels no need to.

When they pick up Larissa at the clinic, she says, "It's going to be rush hour soon."

Mirko holds Larissa's arm gently as they walk back to the car. In some spontaneous harmony, they cross French, Croatian and English sentences between them, content with the loose thread and with not knowing all of what the others are saying. As Mirko helps Larissa get into the car, they both have the patience of good care workers, or wise spouses. And when they let Mira out, at an intersection by the hotel, they appear, at least, cheerful and content. Mirko gets out of the car and holds Mira softly, for a second, next to the curb, before rushing back to catch the light.

SHE IS PLEASED to get back to the hotel and welcomes the musty smell of the entranceway and the withering edges of the flyers pinned to the corkboard, advertising cruises on the Seine. The dining room chairs are neatly pulled in and blocks of sunlight — uneven triangles and cubist rectangles, with curvy plant shadows inside them — fall over the tables. A temporary calm, hiding the state of continual preparation common to hotels and restaurants. How quickly a place fools you into feeling like a home.

In her room, she gently picks up the towel she left on the bed that morning and lets it drop to the floor. There is her phone, too, still on the floor near the pigeon's box.

It rings as she lays it down on the bedside table.

"Mama."

"Mirice moja. I've been calling."

"Are you alright?"

"I'm fine, just fine. Ivan came by to fix the television, and it worked that night, but then it went dead again."

"Oh —"

"But that's fine, I wanted to tell you something else."

"What?"

"You know what I did, instead of watching television, is I went into town, I walked to the centre and sat in the park and had ice cream, and —"

"Is that a little too much walking — were you walking in the rain?"

"Walking is so good for you! Though I did get wet, despite my umbrella and rain jacket. I mean, the bench was in that gazebo — but listen. You know what I saw — all the oaks and chestnuts in the park were full of crows. Dozens of them, so many. Landing on the branches, talking to each other, flying away and flying back. Well, you know how stupid and super-stitious people are about crows — the man next to me on the bench said they gather in the central park, hundreds of them, and isn't it creepy, and mustn't it mean it's the end times?"

Mira sits down and settles in. What was the use in trying to interrupt? She couldn't care about her cell charges right now.

"Well, this is something crows do. I know because your dad and I watched a whole documentary about it. What they do when they aren't nesting, is the flock gathers in the evening and goes to sleep as a flock. But when night falls, all of them, together, fly away to their actual place of rest. And no one will know where that is! That loud gathering in the evening is just a trick, you know, like a biological defense mechanism. Like a survival act. Isn't that something?"

"I suppose. I don't know if I really get it, to be honest —"

Silence on the other end — disappointment, surely?

"I guess there was something else I wanted to tell you.

Ask you. There was a drawing. I think one of you girls drew it. I think it was you. It was a giraffe, but you drew it as if it were standing in our yard, eating the leaves of the oak tree, resting its foot on top of the old septic tank. It was so realistic and detailed but obviously so fantastic — because there could never be a giraffe in our — well, I don't think I threw it out, though you know I chucked most things, but I kept this, and I searched all the drawers and boxes and I wonder, do you know? Do you know about it?"

"Ljilja drew that. She got those new crayons and it was the first thing she drew. But I don't know where it is. I mean, I didn't imagine it was still around."

"Are you sure it wasn't you? You were so good at drawing. Did you want to be an artist or something? I didn't mean to discourage you. I threw things out because I couldn't bear chaos, and kids create so much chaos."

"Mom! An artist, God. I wasn't good at drawing. It was Ljilja."

"But I know I didn't throw that out because it was so perfect."

"Mama. Should we talk tomorrow?"

"It wasn't only order I wanted, you understand, but beauty, and you can't — I never got those back, not really. I do wish I had that drawing — some things of yours — now."

"It's okay. It's okay. My battery will die here. I'll see you tomorrow."

"Okay then —"

Though it hurts her to do it, she hangs up without waiting. The battery is not quite dying, but it is all too much.

She smooths down parts of the duvet with slow hands, and lies down on top of it, shoes and all, putting her hand over the faint wine stain Bernard pointed out on the first day.

She lines up some of the parts: the young woman's green skirt, undulating like the French girl's flawless blouse. That boy the young woman cradled in her lap, a boy who seemed to love being cradled and willing to take all the love coming his way. Mirko's half-sunk apartment. The sharp lemonade, the robust pomegranate. The softness of Mirko's face, with its gentle folds, as he told her how he'd waited for her letter. The park sculpture squeezed by time and gravity.

The back of David's head as he walked toward departures — she had driven him to the airport several times, sure — and his shoulders quivering under the weight of the duffel bag. Her dear dad, in a generic hospital bed, his head turned to the side, mouth slightly open. Mom home alone, flipping impatiently through glossy magazine pictures of actresses on the beach. Eating ice cream on a bench and reminiscing.

If she told her mother about seeing Mirko, if she described everything as it just happened, her mother would say, What a pity. What a pity, what's become of that man. But, Mira thinks, that would be all wrong. And her mother had never liked him, anyway. He was from a working-class family and went to a trade school. Whenever she found Mira talking to him on the phone, she had a reason why the phone line had to be kept free. It was rather like Larissa walking in, interrupting whatever might or might not have been going on.

She had not written to Mirko because she had fallen in love. She'd got away to Canada, and her body was intact, and she was making enough money cleaning hotel rooms to rent a bachelor suite, and she was of sound enough soul to fall in love. How could it be fair? They were two kids when they parted. This is only the beginning of how they will estrange us from one another, Merima had said.

Hello hello, says David, getting swiftly into bed next to her where she's reading, his forehead touching hers, his breath powdery on her cheek. I see you, he says, I see you there pretending to read. Hello hello hello.

There you are. Yes yes. Come in.

Oh that was so long ago.

She should have written back to Mirko, of course. She should have helped him recover some faith in people. She should've, simply, stayed his friend.

As she sinks into the mattress, Mirko vanishes; first he is a ball of yarn in her hands, and then nothing but fluff, and then, though she knows she is in a room in a hotel in Paris, she is also in a swamp that is her own real husband, the man she has really loved and made love to and slept alongside of. She is wearing next to nothing in this swamp, so she pulls more tightly on the duvet, and it smells pungent and dead and fertile in here; everything is damp, the sky soggy and green like the bog—her hair sticks to her sweaty forehead, and this particular strange slough is thick with unidentified stuff, like neon-green moss, which, wait, used to collect on the river that she grew up by;

so she wades through it past a pair of storks, who frighten her with their fragility, those insane stick-legs; she wipes the sweat from her forehead and sees a flash of porcupine, its undulant carpet of quills; unlike the porcupine, she is about as agile as a seal on land, slow and bewildered; now in the distance is a yellow canoe, carried along on the quick North Saskatchewan river, filled with happy, tiny settlers on the Indigenous people's river, faster than she will ever be — just look at her, enraged and sweating, in only a dumb cotton undershirt and panties, a whole lot of something stuck in her throat.

A weird chirpy sound startles her — is it the pigeon?

She doesn't want to get up.

Look where she is: a room as random as any room anywhere.

Oh, but it's not. Bebe followed his heartbreak here and she chose to follow him.

She closes her eyes again, and she is back in her current apartment, inhaling the smell of curry or beef broth spreading through the halls. She was struck, when she first moved there, how she'd walk out to check if the laundry machine was free and be hit with the smell of soup — real dinner, somewhere. She was not cooking then. She sees herself standing at the counter, eating white tortilla wraps rolled into squishy tubes, dipping the ends into the bottom of a jar of Dijon. In that building, she could hear everything: one neighbour's phone ringing late in the evening, another's kitchen drawer shutting with a rattle behind her bed — that was Steve, who never went out, whose light always stayed on. The couple down the hall greeting

their friends, who were thumping up the steps and enthusias-
tically explaining their lateness. On the floor below, the little
girl's pink bike outside the couple's first floor apartment door.
Mira is coming home from an aimless evening walk and looks
into their living room, through the gauzy white curtains, and
sees the mother on the sofa with a hand on her belly, a second
child on the way.

More chirping, and she knows it is her phone, she is in a
hotel room and her phone is on the floor and that is reality.
She can see the pigeon, silent, in a corner of the box.

If David really appeared before her, if just one of the dozens of apparitions she sees turned into the real him, she might
just say, Come home. It's alright. Things have happened, sure,
but we're still here, we're cooking, there'll be stuffed peppers
and home-fried donuts, and you can stay as long as you like.

Come home. But David, David, where was his heart even?
Carried along on some quick or lazy river. Planning a different
homecoming. There is another place I must get to, his heart
calls out, sorry!

It's alright, it's alright.

It had to be this way.

That's what her mother used to say, usually of accidents
and misfortune.

No, it didn't have to be this way, Mira's been saying for years.

But look — that's how it is! So do as you told Mirko to do
years ago, more or less: just wrap it up and put it away. Just
put it away now.

BERNARD'S RIGHT EYE is swollen nearly shut: a remarkably round smooth golf ball, of a deep, tender pink colour. The cheekbone and the eyebrow bone are pink too, the tissue still growing with the blood pooling under the skin. The eye hidden inside the swollen dumpling of tissue and blood and pulsing veins looks out through a very thin opening, straining, red and alarming — and alarmed.

He looks the way others have looked after a beating — shamed, disoriented, and alternately despondent and defiant. His head is bent down and his hands joined in his lap, trembling slightly.

Merima saw Bernard walk through the foyer, dazed and shaking, in the company of an elderly couple, and she stopped him before he climbed the stairs. She took him to the kitchen, looked over his eye, and gave him ice and aspirin.

Mira moves to sit beside him on the bed, because she sees that if she continues to kneel in front of him and look up at his face as she is doing now, he will begin to cry. Seeing his thumbs twitching in his lap, it takes all she has not to cry herself.

"When they punched me, I thought my eyeball was pushed back through my skull. A car drove by, lay on its horn. They kicked me. Then they ran."

Inside her is a deep anxiety, as if she just realized they've been sleeping with the door unlocked and a serial predator, or maybe just one of those voyeurs who likes to steal women's panties and whose violent tendencies are as-yet-unproven, has been operating in the neighbourhood. Why would anyone do this to Bebe?

"Did you see them coming?"

"I just noticed them looking at me, and before I knew it, they were on me. This couple drove me home. They had honked to get these guys to stop. When the guys ran away, they got out of the car."

"What did they look like, the men?"

"That couple said, They probably wanted to rough you up for a few euros. And that's when I thought — that girl."

The pigeon scratches inside the box.

That girl, right, that girl. Mira should've thought of that. Young women who are made to panhandle on the street for a living are probably not free to hang out alone with random tourists who might try to get them back to their room.

Why had he been so naively confident?

Okay, but — be careful, she tells herself.

"It's not your fault," she says as softly as she can. Then, still softly, "How many were there?"

"Two."

"Does it hurt?"

He nods; he is four years old and she finds him on his knees in the gravel in front of the swing, the swing swaying and he frozen. She scoops him up and asks, Did you jump? He nods shyly before starting to wail.

"I think we should go to a clinic —"

"We didn't buy travel insurance."

Sure they didn't — who does?

"Have you talked to your mom or dad yet?"

"Oh God, I can't. Not yet."

"I can call your mom." But she dreads the thought. He's not a child, but still, she feels — how could she have let this happen to him?

"No, I will — just —"

"I'll go down and see about some painkillers, okay?"

She goes in search of the owner, or Merima, or someone in charge. She finds a receptionist, who's already heard someone has come in beaten up, and who calls, for some reason, the Polish man Mira had taken to be a plumber, who in turn advises calling the head of housekeeping, and soon the whole hotel is stirring; maids are appearing from doors Mira never even noticed before, and the story is told again and again, with Mira understanding none of it. Then the owner appears, with Merima, and he already knows everything; it seems, in fact, the couple who dropped Bernard at the hotel delivered the story to him in detail. They'd witnessed it all: a nice-seeming young man minding his own business, blindsided by two thugs.

With everyone talking now, and people texting and even phones ringing, Mira thinks, what are they talking about? And reading her mind, Merima says, "The maids are figuring out who might be a nurse — they overhear things, you know, and notice people's stuff." They land on an English woman on the third floor — old, they say, but a retired nurse.

So they delay the woman's dinner by entreating her to have a look at Bernard: she has no hope of refusing the cavalry that appears at her door. The owner has even dug up a dusty first aid kit.

Mira manages to get the woman to see Bernard alone. She asks him to look right and left, checks his temperature, and asks if he feels dizzy, or perhaps wants to throw up.

"There's no concussion," she says, "but watch for fever. He feels a bit warm to me. Though I don't see other signs of infection. But if you see any pus coming out of that eye, don't you ignore that." She has her grey hair in the kind of curls you get from sleeping in curlers, and her mouth is a thin line of dull red lipstick. She speaks to Mira instead of Bernard, as if he were a child and Mira the adult in charge. She moves back from him a step, considers.

"Poor sod. You've never had a shiner, have you? Well now. By the time you're getting married, you won't remember a thing."

Mira thinks, does everyone everywhere say that?

"Just keep doing ice. And these will help. Two at a time, as you like." She hands Mira a sleeve of small pale green pills.

"Thank you for all this help," Mira says, wishing to hug the woman. Instead, she pets her arm rather awkwardly, and the woman simply says goodbye.

Bernard swallows two pills. Mira wraps a small towel around a fresh bag of ice, which Merima gave her, and he holds it over his eye. She herself would hold that bag of ice on his eye forever, would cradle his head in her arms—but he is not four years old.

There is a lesson in all this, her dad says, his eyes red and watering.

Shut up, she says.

She sits on the armchair, watching him lying there, the ice balanced on his face, his eyes closed. Just as she wonders if he might be falling asleep, he takes the ice off, sits up and grimaces.

"Lie down, sweetheart—"

His good eye twitches and he shakes his head.

She stands up. "What is it?"

"I think you really don't understand about Aisha."

"Oh, don't worry. Please. Rest." She tries to hand him back the ice pack he's laid down next to him on the bed. He waves it away.

"It really wasn't all her fault."

"Okay. That's okay." She still stands by the bed, lays a hand on his shoulder now, gently nudges the ice at him with her other hand.

"Seriously. I've been seeing this counselor. He charges on a sliding scale. He's the one who—can you quit it with the ice?"

She lets the ice pack go.

"He's the one who made me realize I had a problem. That I couldn't stand being alone. I didn't see it then but that's how it — and can you please just sit down?"

When she lowers herself into the armchair again, it sags under her as if she's sat into a hammock.

"He was right. That's how it was. I could never be without her."

Mira watches the ice sitting uselessly on the bed. Couldn't he ice and talk at the same time? If that swelling doesn't go down —

"I didn't often make it home from campus before Aisha, because we tried to match our classes, and when we couldn't, I'd find things to do so we might go home together. You know how I'd sometimes show up at your place with an hour or two to kill?"

What she remembers best are the nights they both visited and happily cooked together. But Bernard dropping in alone — yes, that happened; he'd have a beer then get Aisha's text and jump up to leave.

"But let's say I did beat her home, which happened a handful of times. I'd end up standing by the window, looking down at the bus stop. I would watch for when the number eight would come. I would think, her class ended at four, she would've caught the bus that comes at twenty after, she should be getting off the bus around four thirty-five. But then she might text that she's stopping at the store for shampoo, or she got talking to someone and they'll have a beer. And I couldn't handle it. I mean, it got so I couldn't handle it."

He leans back into the pillow, closes his eyes briefly.

"You didn't trust — sorry to be blunt — you didn't trust that's what she was doing?"

"No. That's not what I mean. She wasn't like that. Or not until the very end. And by then she must've thought about leaving so many times — and when you do, what's there to keep you on course?

"Near the end I got this nervous habit of scratching the backs of my hands. I'd try to do something else, measure water for the rice cooker or chop broccoli, cook up some version of a dish she'd taught me how to make, but I'd just end up back at the window, tearing at my hands. I couldn't stand being inside, and I also couldn't go anywhere, because then she'd come home and I wouldn't be there. Remember you asked me once, do I have eczema?"

"It was winter, and I thought, the dryness, the cold —"

"It didn't really look like eczema."

"Your mom had the same problem —"

"It's okay. Well, one time after I'd waited for her a long time, we had an argument. I ended up kneeling in front of her where she sat on a kitchen chair. I'd got down to pick up some sliced onions that had fallen from the table where she was slicing them, dozens of thin slivers; I was picking them up one by one, and then I stopped and just continued arguing from down there. She turned her chair to face me as she argued back. Back and forth we went, she still turning away to chop every half-minute. And then, somehow, I was holding her hands — just stop cutting already! — and then I was clutching her arms, and then she was done listening to me, clearly, but I wouldn't let her get up. Listen, I kept saying. And I must have pushed hard enough that she got a thin line of a bruise, from where the cheap Ikea metal pressed into her back."

"A bruise? Did you not see that you were pushing that hard?"

He closes his eyes, opens them after a long moment.

"It just seemed so important that I make her understand whatever it was I was making her understand."

"And what was that?"

"I don't really remember."

"You don't even remember."

"No."

"Well, I don't suppose it's the thing that matters."

"I was so ashamed afterwards, I couldn't even touch the bruise, or her — though later we made — anyway, I could not touch her or look at her or beg her forgiveness. I couldn't stand the whole script — weirdo one day, nice guy with flowers trying to make it up the next day. And what the fuck do you do, when you're suddenly that guy? And I couldn't be any other guy but the guy who did that. You see what I'm saying? So what do you do?"

She looks over, more closely, at his hands — smooth, ordinary, only the cuticles somewhat ragged.

"And what did you do?"

He closes his eyes again. "Is that pill supposed to make you sleepy? I feel sleepy."

She leans in toward him. "Hm. I don't really know what those are. I assumed they were something like ibuprofen."

"Not much. I didn't do much. I'm sorry, I'm really sleepy."

His face relaxes. She checks the sleeve of pills, but it's blank, and each pill only has the number 100 stamped into it. When she looks at him again, he's asleep. The ice is melting through its towel onto the duvet, a slowly spreading darkness. She hopes that him being asleep is alright. He seems peaceful, at least, finally, though it must be a brief respite, at best — this is no place to stay.

She sits in the armchair and looks outside. Still afternoon, early, just clouds coming in. When her phone sounds, she moves quickly to silence it, to not wake Bernard. But the name on the screen startles her nearly as much as the first sight of Bernard's eye.

"Hi Mira," the text message begins. "Sorry if this is a little awkward because we haven't talked in a while, but I still have your number. I know you and Bernard are together in Paris, and he's been in touch with me pretty regularly, but now I haven't heard from him for a couple of days, and I know this is a little irrational, but I only wonder if everything is alright? Because I know his grandma is ill, and I'm just a little worried. Sorry to bother you, hope this isn't too weird. All best. Aisha."

For Christ's sake.

All best. A little awkward.

She looks over at Bernard. He hasn't moved.

Dear Aisha, everything is fine, we've been busy sightseeing. Dear Aisha, Bernard got beat up, most likely because he followed around a girl who looked like you. Dear Aisha, how are you, anyway? We miss you.

"I'm not sleeping."

"Oh, for God's sake." She picks up her phone from where it clattered to the ground.

"Just resting."

Of course Aisha knows there is trouble.

Dear Aisha, what is it that you need from Bernard? What have you not forgiven him, or not forgiven yourself? Also, we have this pigeon. How is one supposed to know when it's ready to fly?

Just put it outside and see if it flies.

Okay, but — have you really forgiven Bernard? Are you actually taking some weird, very passive revenge? How much is there to avenge, anyway?

"Who's texting you?"

"Just a dumb email. How're you feeling?"

He sits up, then stands up, slowly. Goes to the mirror over the sink.

"Looks bad, doesn't it?" He sticks his face very close to the mirror, and moves his head just perceptibly — slightly up, slight left, down. She thinks, that's brave, to assess the whole painful, inflamed mess so minutely.

He's been at it for what seems a long time, when they hear a gentle knock.

He pulls back from the mirror, looks at Mira. Then takes two steps and opens the door.

Mira can't quite see who it is.

"I tried your door, but then figured you must be with your aunt. What an awful thing to happen."

"Oh, that's so nice of you," she hears Bernard say, as he steps into the hallway, not quite closing the door behind him.

Hm. She looks out through the balcony. She thinks of what she's felt but hated to think of—the girl Bernard had talked to, Janina, maybe the very same one she watched play with rocks in the park, even though Mirko said her name is Klementina. If this really had to do with her, then who knows what happened to her? And if they slapped her or beat her or something else— punched her so that her eye has swelled up into a red mess— well, there'd have been no nice elderly couple to escort her to safety, no army of hotel residents checking on her bruises and giving her sympathy. Maybe there'd have been no sympathy at all.

She hears, "Well, I just wanted to make sure that you're alive."

In a moment, Bernard steps back inside and closes the door gently. "That was Alice. She's so nice."

"The American girl?" What a concerned soul, after nothing but a one-night stand. And how easily Bernard accepts that women just come around, sympathetic, taking care of him.

She looks out again, away from him. "Everybody is so nice. Like that French girl. Selma?"

"Yeah, Selma."

"And what was the name of the girl who works here I saw you with outside the hotel?"

He picks up the sloppy wet towel from the duvet. "I wonder if I should get more ice from downstairs."

"Bebe. Is pinning Aisha to a chair really the worst thing you've ever done?"

When she says it, he shocks her: he colours up, from his throat up into his cheeks, something she cannot remember ever seeing on him, a slow progression he seems helpless over, wet towel in his hands, his bruise deepening, the blush flaming. He blinks rapidly with his one good eye as if he were trying to clear something out of it. He lets the towel drop, and before his eye can well over, he turns and leaves the room.

And she immediately regrets it. As if she has accidentally deleted a very important piece of text — this has happened at work, sure — she thinks, against rising panic, I can still undo, click the back arrow on the toolbar. It can't be that she has driven him away like this — at the worst moment — oh, it was too thoughtless of her.

She knocks softly on his door and speaks in the self-deprecating, light, deflecting tone their family uses in tense situations, a tone with a specific mid-range colour, roomy, spoken from the back of the throat, gentle but lively.

"Don't be mad at your stupid aunt," she says.

But he does not respond. She brings herself to knock once more.

"Are you in there, Bebe?" Already her voice sounds strained and desperate, and she keeps calling him Bebe, a childhood name she stopped saying aloud some years ago.

She walks quickly down the stairs, fleeing, again, as this morning.

WITH RELIEF HE hears Mira's footsteps on the stairs. Alone.

After he came back from his run, the evening of the broken-winged pigeon, he first saw the feathers strewn all around the parking lot. Upstairs, Aisha was casual, slipping out of her pants — "You could've just brought it up, put it in a shoe box on the balcony" — heading into the shower. The fucking showers at random times. He followed her around as she danced away from him, "Do you think it was already dead when the others, you know, started pecking it?" His flaccid voice, ugh, no wonder she was always half-turning away from him. Then she's undoing her bra, sweet sharp elbows, little bumps of her spine; "Well, close to dead, probably," as if it didn't matter. Her purple blouse and those elastic-waist pants she always wore laid out on the bed, God, he loved her: the hair on her forearms, her gums when she smiled. Then the shower water running, he sitting alone on the bed, his salty lips, dry mouth, something was *wrong*, something was entirely inadequate, what was it? Her purse a sudden target, innocently slouching on the floor by the bed, covered sloppily by her cardigan, the holder of things, what things? Her phone not in the front pocket, but at the bottom, under makeup and a small notebook — he disturbed all of that, why not, because once he'd unzipped the top zipper he was already doing this thing, was already in, not even thinking how he'd cover his tracks. A text thread with someone whose name he didn't know, a dumb name of indefinite gender, the texts brief and terse; then he's in the photos, folders within folders, which he opens nervously and quickly, until he taps one that makes him throw the phone down. The shower water stops — he notices it has stopped, anyway. The door creaks open and he moves toward it. "Did you drop some —" she begins, holding the door partly open, adjusting the towel under her armpit, and he raises his hand.

What had he been thinking, as he raised his hand? This hand here, lying peacefully on the reddish duvet, no longer trembling. You weren't thinking, said his counselor, you were reacting. But it was a murky humiliation, wasn't it? At having been an idiot about the pigeon? Thinking Aisha would care? Or at having been a fool in this other way that he couldn't yet measure?

The sweat from his run had cooled off and there were patches of clamminess all over his body, his spine a cold riverbed. His socks tight at the ankles. After a run he usually, in a kind of exhilaration, peeled off everything immediately.

This time he remembers how the clothes stayed on, a stiff, heavy, tight costume, long after Aisha left the apartment and even as he lay in bed, seeing traces of dawn outside.

WHAT FOR TWO DAYS has been an ongoing breeze is now a genuine wind. The streets are socked in. And you with nothing to cover your head, she hears her father's voice. But she has no retort in her this time.

Bernard's hurt face reminds her of a painful scene from her teenage years, involving a boy she liked: a serious boy who got teased by others because he was intellectual and loud about it, but whom everyone still liked because, tall and quick, he was reliable for nightly games of basketball. Another boy got into an argument with him over his oral exam in history class that day—this other boy said, "You were getting a hard on talking about the battle of the Turks."

And as the boy she liked turned his back on the taunt, the other one pulled down his shorts. There for all to see was the tall boy's bum, plump and milky white, like buns their mothers made on Sunday morning, doughy and bursting out of the pan before they were slid into the oven. A child's bum, cartoonish, vulnerable, comical, a caricature of spanking comics.

His face reddened so much that it seemed to swell up and he blinked his eyes until tears nonetheless slid down his cheeks. It took him a moment to pull his shorts up and scream, "You're so stupid!" After that he stopped talking to Mira. She had, like the others, simply sat silent and pitying him as he walked away.

Forgive me, she says.

And that is when she sees him, sitting on the low brick fence separating the sidewalk from a courtyard — not that boy, nor Bernard, but Dad, her dad, her dead father.

"What, you haven't missed me," he says, sitting there like a loitering kid, wearing his slightly oversized dress pants and suede Adidas running shoes and a checkered short-sleeve shirt. His hands are clasped loosely in his lap; she can see the age spots on his large-knuckled hands.

The lump inside her chest cavity twitches. How much can be expected of that mushy, restless tissue? Does God know what he's doing to her heart, when he whacks it like this: Dad, hanging out, looking sweet and in the mood to tease?

But she keeps very still, stares at him, the way you try to keep yourself in a dream that threatens to dissolve.

He looks much the same. Quite sprightly. Once a very old woman, a neighbour of Mira's grandmother, called him "this boy." Ha, he'd laughed, a boy of sixty-five! Why to die then, still looking so much as if belonging to life, with a real living appetite for collecting suede shoes, many chess games to play with his grandson, and a newfound enthusiasm for trying every latest superfood smoothie recommended by the internet?

He does look well, only maybe his shirt is somewhat hollow in the chest area, where so much pumping took place.

The thing about Dad is, he became really soft sometime after sixty. He was gentle with their mom, for instance, next to whom he would sit for hours, on the couch, with his hand placed lightly on her middle back, watching penguins on television waddle in a one-penguin formation over some snowy hill in Antarctica, getting teary eyed when the penguins were shown protecting their young or exhibiting other acts of devotion. They mate for life, he would say, holding up his index finger. Occasionally he would get as excited by footage of a snake swallowing, slowly, a whole crocodile. But what seemed to enthuse him most were the portrayals of sacrifice and integrity among the polar bears and giraffes and koalas.

What has become of you, Mira's mother had said, at first. But soon she settled into it. They got a super high-tech bread maker and together they mixed breads with strange seeds and unusual kinds of flour; when Dad mixed a hard bread, which he often did, liking to free-wheel it, Mom, getting into the new approving spirit of things, said, "It's not too hard, that bread, just a hearty peasant bread."

And Dad stood patiently by Bernard on the badminton court, at the sporting club on the outskirts of town, where Bernard spent many an afternoon of his summer vacations in Croatia — Dad would guide his arm up to show the full extent of the swing necessary for a solid serve, with Bebe occasionally stomping his feet in impatience and frustration. "Now, son,"

Dad would say, "don't worry so much. How long do you think it took me to learn?"

(He may not have been this patient with Mira and her sister; possibly there had been less-than-gentle elbow guiding, accusations of laziness, and long lectures, on the way home from the courts, about being, in terms of athleticism, complete embarrassments.)

"The thing I wanted to tell you," he starts now, "is that I'm sorry if—"

"Oh, for God's sake, don't," she says. She looks around for people who might see or hear her — she has spoken aloud. Could others see him? He is a vivid, autonomous entity, which, nonetheless, will dissolve, she fears, if some careless passerby here in the real-world coughs too loudly.

"The thing is, there is so much you don't know in the moment it would help you to know it. We didn't talk about our feelings a lot. Mostly I thought, when your mother was in a rage, I should get out of her hair and go to the club to play chess. And no one talked about how you should treat your kids. You just had kids, and they were either good or bad. Not like your sister, reading books about how to calm your kid's tantrum by telling him to smell an imaginary flower. We thought tantrums should be smacked out of a kid! You were mostly good kids. Girls were more often than boys. Although girls could be real hellions too, remember that little curly-haired — well, it doesn't matter. What I think now is, maybe things could've been different. I just wanted you to know."

A woman passes Mira on the sidewalk, soft-footed, in-different.

When the woman seems out of earshot, Mira says, "Do you gain special skills when you're up there?"

"What happens on the other side is that things become a little clearer. Certain delusions fall away. Like the one that your mother didn't do it with that asshole neighbour when we visited their cottage. She did do it and more than once and she did lie her face off about it. What also happens is that you feel more confident people can take the truth," he says. He pries Mira's hand off her stomach and holds it in his own hands. They feel like warm air around her skin.

"I miss the Adriatic," he says. "The way it blows salt on every-thing. And how you girls' hair would be full of it after a day of swimming, and I couldn't get my hand through it when I tried. I miss coming into a house smelling of coffee. I miss how you could learn a thing — a new chess opening you couldn't have imagined before — and how I would think, this too is possible. I don't miss that prick of a neighbour. I still have to see him sometimes, even here. I miss Bebe. Tell him that I —"

Coldness, suddenly — he's dropped her hand to press on his own chest cavity.

And with that he is gone.

She has to jump up to manage it, but she sits on the wall herself. There is no warmth, no shadow, where he just sat, noth-ing at all. A boy passes by without looking her way.

Oh Lord, you who cast low and raise up also.

235

She went to what they called a classical high school where you learned Latin and philosophy, and though she remembers next to squat, really, of Greek and Roman mythology, one story stuck, probably because it affronted her: Orpheus and Eurydice. All that effort he goes to, to bring her back from the underworld — only to lose her again and watch her float away from him when he breaks the decree not to look back as he leads her out.

She looks down at her hand, which the apparition had made her move off her stomach, so he could hold it in his own two hands.

It doesn't surprise her, that he'd come like this, unanticipated, on a street in Paris, contradicting his — and her! — skepticism about sightings of the dead.

Of course, she could not have led him out.

She looks through her purse, finds crumbs, a hard corner of baguette, not ideal, headache pills, a tiny calendar, the useless refill of a lost pen, and finally — maybe that will do — some candy. Cough candy, oval and cherry-flavoured, with one of those oozing centres. She unwraps that and puts it on the wall.

She knows enough to leave food for the dead, something, if possible, resembling a heart.

Then she climbs down self-consciously, smooths the seat of her pants, and walks away, conscious of not looking back.

Suddenly the wind picks up so much that a gust of it drives dirt into her eyes and nose. A second gust makes her stand still for balance, the gravel whipping her bare legs and arms.

A child's bike helmet is blown along the sidewalk, tumbling like a watermelon, with loud, hard *thunk*s. The sky is a sodden blanket, swollen and grey, and in a moment's time, the rain starts, in quick, fat drops.

The storm is a loose beast. Thick streams pour down eaves, gurgle fast down drainpipes; in the road, lakes form and are heaved by the wind, and in a quick minute her pants are pasted to her thighs, her feet smacking wetly against her drenched shoes with each step. Water pours behind her ears and down her neck.

She runs into a shop, where the bell above the door announces her entrance. Turns out it is the worst kind of shop to be in when you can't move an arm without spraying water: a tiny fine stationery shop. The young woman behind the counter — a mere two metres away from the door — measures her silently.

"Pardon, pardon." Mira feels streams of water weave down her back and legs but there is not a thing she can do; she lifts her hand to wipe her face, but her dripping elbow comes rudely close to a swivel stand displaying hand-drawn postcards of Paris bridges at dusk. On her other side is a table display of small and large watercolours, and she is a melting column in the middle, with nowhere to turn.

Then, remarkably, the woman says, in English, "What rain, suddenly, no?" She looks down, moves her hand through a drawer, comes up with a small packet of tissue.

"Please," she says, pulling one out halfway and extending it to Mira.

Oh lord. Mira takes one and wipes her face.

"Thank you." She crumples the tissue into her purse.

"Look around," the woman says, "wait it out."

The place is well-lit and done in soft colours, whites and ivories and greys. At the far end of the display table, otherwise taken up largely by watercolours of the Luxembourg Gardens, is a series of small postcards, each card a detailed hand-drawing of a single pigeon. They are rendered in colour ink, with complicated, unbroken line work, and strange hyper-realness. Each is different: one dark grey and with the familiar scaly green sheen at the neck that seems to rise from the paper — much like the real pigeon she has been looking at for two days now; another one with a white underbelly blending into a soft pink, with the pink giving way to light grey at the wings. The colours somehow hover above the paper, but the whole figure has the depth of embroidery and seems both heavy and intricate.

Mira stares at these cards, her hands at her sides.

The pigeons' heads angle so that they look here pensive, there alert and vigilant.

As if they are longing, even, which surely must be beyond their capability.

She checks her fingers for dryness and holds up one card gingerly, the one of the dark grey pigeon like the bird in her room.

"These are the most beautiful things I have ever seen," she says.

"Oh!" The girl waves her hand in dismissal. "Those are mine. I mean, I do those."

Why does this send prickles of joy through Mira, as if she'd come across a wild orchid or an outcrop of colourful mushrooms on an ordinary walk home?

She looks up. "You don't really?"

The girl looks slightly uncertain for a moment.

"Oh! I do, yes."

Keep it together, try not to smile so wildly. But she can't help it. "Something amazing just happened to me."

The girl raises her eyebrows. She is a pale girl, with woolen blondish hair. "What was it?"

It is not at all Mira's habit to speak this way, but inside her chest is a cleaving motion, something fast and lively and cheerful moving through her, independent of her conscious will. Still, she stops herself. Says instead, "The thing is, I have a pigeon in my hotel room right now. Its wing was broken — I found it on the street and brought it up."

"Poor thing."

"I put it in a box — with some crumbs and such, you know. It looks much like this pigeon. I mean not as beautiful, but —"

"How is it doing?"

"Fine? I think. How can you know?"

"It's eating?"

"Eating, yes. Moving about."

"Well, then —"

"Probably fine, right?"

"I'm sure."

Self-consciousness moves in. Without looking for the price, Mira says, "I will buy this one."

It turns out the drawing is expensive, but here is her credit card, a marvellous invention. After the girl rings the card through, she does something else — from a drawer in the desk where the register sits, she pulls out another, smaller card, with a drawing of a sparrow.

"If you like this one too," she says, "take it as a gift."

She does like it, because pigeons and sparrows were the two humble, unappreciated birds of her childhood. And though only black and white, and plainer and looser in its line work so that the bird doesn't have the same density, it too is beautiful.

"I couldn't — it's too much."

"Nonsense," the girl says, "they are just little cards." She places both in tissue, then brown paper sleeves, then a plastic bag.

A man walks into the store. Looking past him through the windows, Mira sees that the storm has spent most of its power, already, though minutes ago it seemed relentless. She lets the man take her place inside — there is hardly room for more than one person at a time.

Closing the door behind her, holding her gift, she thinks, Let no one ever tell me the French are haughty.

Inside her chest is again a brisk happy scythe, swinging about. Somewhere nearby, still in the Latin Quarter, she ambles into another park; here, the treetops are joined in a fluffy, uneven canopy, and the sky is now a liquid grey-blue, with clouds chugging past. She has looked up at trees and clouds hundreds of times, in the same self-consciously search-ing way. Down below, a light scraping sound: a dog, with a mangy, shaggy coat, trailing a large greasy paper wrapper stuck to its behind. The dog sniffs casually along the ground, then twists its head as if to look at the paper. Suddenly it gives a decisive, full body shake, and the wrapper dislodges. The dog goes on, poking and smelling about. She thinks: the rulers of the world oppress their citizens and non-citizens and target consumers in many ways, but in the matter of grief and love they are not, fully, the lords. She is rehearsing something that, when it comes, might even feel easy.

When she leaves the park, for a minute she doesn't know where she is, but on reaching the first corner of the street, she looks to her right and recognizes Rue des Écoles: she has felt lost, but she is just a block behind the hotel.

I have been a fool, of course, in more ways than one. I have been a doubting fool, like Orpheus.

She walks quickly up the six flights of stairs. She knocks on the door of Bernard's room without shame. She doesn't say "I'm sorry," through the closed door, only, in her own normal voice, "I love you."

MIRA'S BEEN SITTING on the floor in the hallway for a while, leaning her back against the wall. It's okay, she's got time. She's got time until at least breakfast tomorrow. Only one person has walked by her in the hallway but didn't give her a second look. Sometimes people are curious, yes, but sometimes they just don't want to know.

Little Bernard. One day, in that beautiful museum garden she was reminded of yesterday when she sat in the Luxembourg Gardens, they were eating croissants from the museum café on a bench outside, she and Bebe, talking about the beetle he had just got to hold, plucked out of its glass box and delivered gently by a museum guide into Bebe's palm. She had chosen a spot with shade, because he didn't like to be in the sun. The benches were spaced around rectangular beds of petunias, inside of which were concentrically arranged half-moon beds of lamb's ear and marigolds and more petunias. And in the very middle a concrete clearing, with a circle of brown brick marking the centre spot.

She can see her own youth, her jean shorts and skinny wrists. Hear the bumblebees in the bush next to them, see the ant colony on the ground. And Bernard crouching down, fascinated by the ants' work, trying to intercept them with an extended finger, squealing in delight. "Have a bite," she'd say, every few minutes, and then he'd rise and lean on her knees to eat a piece of croissant.

A cloud passed in front of the sun. And Bebe turned to her suddenly and said, "When the sun is behind a cloud, I can run! Okay? I will run."

And he did, in a straight line heading for the brown-brick circle in the middle. There he turned and waved at her, a rather small boy in the distance. And then he sprinted back. "I beat the sun," he said, wide-eyed back at the bench, as the garden was once again flooded by sunlight. Another bite of croissant, another cloud, and he was off again. A second time, and a third, and a fourth. Watching him run, his skinny, fragile-looking legs, his sandals on loosely because he didn't like them tight, she thought, we might have a tumble here, and the afternoon will be done. But then — that's the worst that can happen, a tumble, scraped knees, and we go home.

She didn't want it to end, didn't want him to cry, but still, it was alright.

He was headed for another round when two young women walked across the lawn toward the flower beds: one dressed in a draping purple gown, with hair braided in a circle around her head, the other in a short jean jumpsuit, carrying a camera.

The woman in the gown held up the corners of the dress and walked lightly in bare feet. Her shoulders were round and white. She and the photographer chatted, laughed, as if self-conscious. Bebe, standing solemnly in the centre now, stared at them. The one in the purple set herself by a bed of yellow marigolds and the photographer crouched, aimed her lens up, then moved a little, laughing. "We don't want the boy in the shot, do we," she said.

Mira could hear the words carried across the garden, as if they were all in a quiet valley where you could hear for miles. Bebe looked up, and, probably thinking he's got some good time left with the cloud cover, he called out to Mira: "Now I'm going to run all the way around. All the way. Okay? Over there." He was both excited, testing himself, and asking permission.

"I'll be here," she yelled back. There was nowhere else she needed to be. And once again he was booting it along, now going around the perimeter instead of in a straight line back to her, running faster, racing against the sun.

He got to her breathless and proud of himself.

"You ran far," she exclaimed.

"I was brave," he agreed.

When she offered him the last bite of croissant, he moved her hand away and said, "Let's go home now." He wasn't upset, just done. So they walked across the grass, past the girls, to the parking lot and the car, where he fell asleep, as always, on the ride home.

The door of his room opens; Mira stands up. He looks crumpled and confused.

"Did you knock earlier?"

"I knocked."

"I thought I heard something, through a dream. I was napping. It was good."

She can see the pillow creases on his cheek.

"You slept through a storm."

"Is that why you're wet? You were out in it?"

She nods.

"You know — that pigeon, that crazy bird," he says. "What are we going to do with it?"

"Do you want to come see? Maybe it's fine now."

They cross into her room, to the box in its same old place, by the balcony. There he is, the pigeon, circling slowly, shifting his weight, like a portly grandmother.

Bernard says, "I don't think it can fly."

"Should we take him to a vet? Actually" — she remembers something — "let's put it on the balcony and see if it flies away."

"Just like that?"

Bernard carries the bird out and releases it slowly on the ground. It immediately tries, flutters, but it gets only human-hip-height. Just short of clearing the balcony railing. Then it just does some walking laps. Bernard keeps watching it as if willing it to fly away. No dice.

So he scoops it up and sets it back into the box.

He sits down on the edge of the bed. "Well."

"Well," Mira echoes, equally perplexed at how to leave behind the creature they were supposed to have saved.

"I was watching these crazy videos earlier" — he taps at his phone — "of receding glaciers. Have you seen this?" She leans over and sees a smooth grey-white surface retreating in speeded up animation. He swipes his forefinger, gets another video, this time an underwater view of plastic floating through the bottom of an ocean.

"Which ocean is that?"

He doesn't answer, swipes again, and now they're watching a time-lapse video of the Arctic's oldest ice shrinking over the last twenty-five years.

He moves to swipe again, but she touches his hand gently.

"Let's not," she says, "there's no point, like this."

He gives in, drops the phone.

"Aisha used to say, Let's not be like the magpies. She'd say it just how you said that now, with the same soft tone, Let's not."

"What did she think of pigeons?"

"Not much. They shit on our car a lot, perched on the power lines above. The night that I'd come across that pigeon in the alley — by the time I came back from my run, it had been pecked at so much that its entrails were spilling onto the ground. It hadn't occurred to me they'd have the same stippled skin under their feathers as chickens."

"Hm."

"Aisha said, why didn't you just bring it upstairs? We'd have put it on the balcony, and it would either die or get better."

"Very simple."

"That was the night I found that stupid video. I looked through her purse while she was in the shower. And when she came out, I swung at her."

"Like —"

"Yes."

"And —"

"She didn't move away, just stood there, wide-eyed. As if ready, even willing, to let it all play out up to its ugliest climax."

"And did you actually —"

"I dropped my arm."

He buries his swollen face in his hands, brings his head low.

"But what's even the difference?" He speaks very quietly behind those hands, in a voice not entirely his own, soft and cratered.

"I guess that's beyond me. But I think there's a difference. Most likely, there is."

"And she felt so guilty about the, you know, she forgave me on the spot, again. She'd have forgiven almost anything, probably. I mean, she was like that. Blamed herself."

"She is a woman, I suppose."

"Maybe she didn't even know what she was forgiving. Do you think?"

She picks up her phone from the armchair and scrolls through texts. "Here," she says, "you can read this." He finally lifts his head, takes the phone from her hand, reads the text Aisha sent her that morning.

"Jeez. Jeez. Did you write back to her?"

"Just in my head. As usual." After a pause she says, "David and I used to tell each other this line — it's from that song — you know I hardly listened to music before I met David? But the line goes something like, If no one's around when your soul departs, I'll go with you into the dark. I wish —" she pauses again. "That I'd got to say goodbye to Aisha."

"Oh don't." When she looks at him, tears run quickly down the sides of his face, into his ears and around his earlobes, down his neck.

Let's not, she would like to say, in the gentlest voice known to humans and angels, but it is a voice she has not formed yet. And let's not what?

"It's okay, Bebe," she says, only approximating the voice of rarified grace, of heavenly consolation.

He weeps as quietly as water runs over rock. She is reluctant to touch him but eventually she covers his one hand softly with her own. Tiny ball of child.

When she hands him a tissue, he wipes quickly around his neck and swipes at the snot under his nose. He balls up the tissue and lobs it away from himself without looking.

"I can't believe this has happened. We never should've come to Paris. How does the rest of the song go?"

"I don't think I can remember. Something about heaven and hell."

"I don't want to go tomorrow. It's too much. I can feel my pulse in this eye. I keep counting the beats, like I'm meditating.

But is that meditating, paying attention to the pain, or should I be, like, putting the pain on the carriage of a train and watching the train carry it away? Or are they the same?"

"I'm sorry. I don't know. Maybe we can book another night here. Though Grandma's waiting for us."

"No, it's okay. It's okay, I'll go."

He shifts to lie on his side, his hands innocently clasped under his good cheek, like a child's in prayer. He touches his fingertips very lightly to the skin under and above his eye.

They've been on the lookout for pus in the eye, for fever, for changes in vision — but there is only pain.

"Do you need another ice pack?"

"I don't think so."

He is thinking of what he felt when the guy first shoved him, the warm hand, the tree bark, the knowledge someone actually meant him harm.

"No one's ever hit me before." He was embarrassed to admit this. Shouldn't he have been in a schoolyard fight, or something? "I got pushed in a bar once. That's it. I never thought — I just didn't imagine — the feeling of this. Like, what are you worth? Nothing, to those people."

"Yes."

"And to think I — I made Aisha feel this way — or some micro-percentage of this."

Mira pauses. "What I meant to say earlier was that, maybe, you've just got to find your own way into the dark — or through the dark."

You can't look for a woman to save you, she didn't add. Bernard doesn't look at her, but she continues.

"Aisha's got her guy — what's his name?"

"His name? What does it matter?"

"Just in so far as he's a real person." People can take the truth, sometimes.

"Robert."

"Well. There. Bebe?"

"I'd rather not. Make my own way."

She waits a little while, then says, "So did your girl wear a long green skirt? The girl you talked to in Montmartre?"

"I don't think so. It was more of a brown, checkered sort of skirt. What does it matter?"

"A girl in a green skirt led me to Mirko. Or that's what I would like to think. But even with such extraordinary guidance — I mean, things are not entirely clear."

"How did she lead you to him?"

"I followed her through the city, and when she stopped, he was there with her. He just appeared in front of me."

"Did you talk to him?"

"We had a really good talk — we spent the afternoon together."

Bernard looks at her as if it's occurring to him for the first time — "Were you in love with him? Like, are you wanting to get back together with him?"

"No. I mean, I was in love with him then. Now I wanted to recover something amid all the lost things." She pauses again.

"But it seems to me now that you can be handed a small miracle, and then you've still got to do the work."

She knew she was talking to herself now. She had to stop being a child at the side of the road, waiting for a parent or friendly neighbour to take her home. When she imagined getting to Mom's place, then calling her friend at the English language school, as she had promised to do when she arrived, and later putting on some slacks, driving in her rent-a-car to a meeting or an interview over there, it seemed farfetched. Ditto when she imagined setting up her few things in the guest room with the rose patch view and making her and Mom's breakfast before going off to teach. She'd have to wipe that counter very thoroughly before leaving, that's for sure.

Maybe what she had to give her mom was this, what she was doing right now — visiting, checking in, arranging. Or — maybe something would change when she landed, walked the familiar streets, saw the familiar walls. When she saw Mom again. She could stay open to that.

"I also saw your grandpa. Just hanging out in a park, telling me he misses life."

"No shit?"

"He told me to tell you he loves you."

She sees him deciding not to question her.

"I miss him, that's for sure," he says.

He also thinks he'd rather not be in his grandparents' house tomorrow, remembering Grandpa, and also explaining to his grandma what happened. He'd rather not leave this hotel room at all. To think of them pulling their suitcases through the streets, then descending underground to take the train to the airport, with all the people in the subway — anything could happen. He wanted to stay here, where the door could lock and someone made you breakfast. "I feel so safe with you," Aisha had said to him, forever ago, while they made out in an underused corner of the university library. Safe.

Her phone buzzes at almost the same time as Bernard's; their phones are always signaling, alerting them, a fog of ciphers. Bernard reaches for his.

"Oh. It's Mom." He hands it to her. Ljilja writes without preamble: "Did you hear about the flooding at home?"

"I've heard about rains and the floods across the border," she says to him, "but—"

He Google searches and quickly pulls up news releases about floods in southeastern Croatia forcing thousands out of their homes.

"I mean, I just talked to Mom, didn't I, and she didn't say—" They read. Mira dials her mother's number. It rings and rings, each time she calls, again and again.

AT SEVEN A.M. in a Paris budget hotel people eat baguettes and canned fruit. They might be thinking of the Picasso museum — which day to visit? — or of ungrateful children who are not answering their phone calls, or, with a shudder, of the humiliation they've had to suffer to secure these two weeks of precious time in Europe, now slipping steadily through their fingers.

At breakfast, Bernard's head hurts in an unfamiliar way, a pressure that seems to move from the base of his skull to the top of his head. The dining room is too bright. People clink and chew and drag their chairs loudly and carelessly.

The night before, Mira phoned everyone whose number she could find and who she thought would forgive her for the late-night phone call. But many people had given up their land lines and she didn't have their cell numbers. She eventually got through to Anica, who told her they weren't under evacuation orders yet, but they may well be in a day or two. She had gone to stay with her daughter west of town, just yesterday, and she had asked Leonarda to come along. "Your mother said she's waiting for you. I couldn't convince her. We told her we'd wait for her to pack up her important things, and she could've phoned you to tell you where she is, but she sent me away."

It was six a.m. when her mom answered the phone. The cell had been silenced and sitting in a place Leonarda could not remember leaving it, she said — the kitchen junk drawer with grocery bags and elastics and pencils.

"It's not as bad as they're saying. They like to exaggerate everything on the news." Then she said, "Is the water safe to drink? From the tap? Do you think?"

Mira put her palm to her temple. She didn't know. "What have you got at home, have you got enough to eat, to drink?"

"I've got enough. Don't worry. I'll be as fine here as anywhere."

"You should've gone with Anica. Her daughter might still pick you up if I ask her. Then we could —"

"I'm sorry, I can't. I've got things to do at home. I did find that drawing, and there are other things I have to find, and — I do hope you come. I've been wanting to talk to you."

Mira thinks now she should've yelled at her, good and fierce: You're sick! You're not fit! Do what I tell you! But then again, to accuse her of infirmity was the worst approach. She'd just double down. And if she tried gentleness — this isn't like the war, Mom — she'd get contempt in return. You think I'm a fool? You think I don't know the difference between a war and a flood?

So, Mira's decided, they will get on their flight, and then rent a car, drive home, and figure it out from there. They'll be there by evening. If they're lucky, nothing worse will happen by evening.

256

In the dining room now, Mira watches a girl — three, four years old — trying to spread Nutella on half a baguette with a spoon. She has a long, messy, strawberry-blond braid hanging down her back. She's making small headway with the Nutella, spackling the bread, when her mother takes the spoon away and pushes a cup of hot cocoa at her.

"Hurry up now."

Mira can see clearly that the drink steams furiously.

"It's hot," says the kid, but still, she tries to lift the cup. She can't seem to lift it, so she lowers her head to meet it, and as soon as her mouth makes contact, she jerks her head back and drops the cup loudly on its saucer, the cocoa spilling, and the girl bringing a hand to her lips, waving it quickly in front of her face, looking scared.

"Wah, wah, wah," says the mother, blotting the spill with a napkin. "Wah wah. Why didn't you blow on it?"

That's when Mira suddenly knows: it's the voice behind the wall that kept her up, the voice she woke up to again and again before she rose and went out into the streets and found Mirko. It was as bad as she thought. What kind of a person? Preventing poisoning, choking, scalding — weren't these the basics?

Merima walks over and briskly, without a word, takes away the hot chocolate. The mother keeps talking quietly to the girl in that droning voice, which seems to have a frequency, like purring. She stops when Merima returns with a cup of chocolate milk, but doesn't look up to acknowledge her. The girl slumps in her chair, her hands folded against her chest, her jaw set forward, eyes walled up, her baguette untouched.

Merima stops at Mira and Bernard's table.

"I hate that woman. She stays here every few months. I don't know why. She's obviously not a tourist. And who even brought a steaming drink to that kid?"

The girl lifts her leg and uses the toe of her dirty pink sneaker to push away the milk in front of her on the table. Mira worries — what kind of rage will ensue now? The child has the concentration of an assassin in pushing that cup, millimetre by millimetre. But her mother, remarkably, is now working hard to shorten the belt on her purse, muttering, it seems, only to herself.

Merima says again, "Did you see who carried that drink over? It wasn't my son, was it?" They both stare at her, as if they still can't take the question seriously. "Well. The trouble of it is you can see the girl might not turn out too well, either."

Sure, you could see the girl becoming obstinate, acting out her rage against school friends and men who will hold her in contempt, throwing all her ugly self-pity out into the world. Becoming, in short, someone it will be hard to pity, to befriend, to love. But then again, she might not. She might already be fencing in, among the chaos and wilderness, a small safe space for herself, an improvised garden in which she will live, for a while.

In any case, Mira won't see this formation, one way or the other. Not for this girl, and not for any other girl. Or boy. She will not be anyone's early wound nor haven.

But she got to see Bernard grow up. Here he is, a real human!

Bernard says, "Did you see that story about that old lady who canoes around her flooded village delivering bread to people? Seriously."

She's seen that story a million times since last night. Some plucky creature. For a moment, Mira wonders if that's the kind of folksy glory her mother might like for herself.

She sees the girl drink some of her chocolate milk. While the mother is distracted, now actually stitching the strap to the purse, with a real needle and thread, the girl carefully, slowly lifts the cup — a small cup, three-quarters full, intended to make drinking possible, obviously — and takes quick, large gulps.

Mira refills her and Bernard's coffees from the urn on the table, because this day will be long.

Then the American family fills out the hallway, their suitcases and backpacks spilling around the reception counter.

"Howdy," Mira hears the dad say to Merima, who has gone to help them. "Time for us to check out."

Alice is the first to look at Mira and Bernard and raise her hand in greeting. But she's already said a real goodbye to Bernard before breakfast.

Something is unnerving about them. They're not smiling. The mother looks tired, although patient. Ditto the brother. Mira can't not stare at them. Yes, these are the dull faces of those in limbo.

"You're going home," Bernard calls out, as if he didn't know that already. He would love to walk over, hug Alice, shake her mom's hand, pat her dad on the back. But he's embarrassed.

The mother waves but does not speak. There is gentleness in the gesture. Maybe that's what she still has to give — to them, to this life.

Alice sighs, spreads her hands in resignation.

Mira thinks, Then again, the dull faces of limbo are also the innocent faces of those patiently waiting for entry.

"I hope your eye gets better soon," Alice calls out. There are only a few empty tables separating them.

"We're leaving today too," Bernard says, presumably for the benefit of her parents.

The father tucks a credit card into a leather wallet shiny from wear and looks at Mira and Bernard across the room as if they are old acquaintances.

"Well, it has to end sometime." He speaks loudly, and touches a hand to his ball cap, as Mira saw him do in the Luxembourg Gardens yesterday.

"You folks have a safe trip. Was a pleasure to know you." He looks at them, as if, somehow, he will really miss them. He pauses for a moment, nods again. Then he takes his wife's hand. There is a circle of waves and, yes, smiles, and a lingering look between Alice, who trails behind, and Bernard. They file out, and there they are, standing on the sidewalk, just on the other side of the window. Mira and Bernard watch through the glass until a taxi pulls up. When it does, the driver gets out, and

immediately looks disgruntled, pointing to them and the suitcases — it's too much, they're too big, how will it all fit? But then
they start working on the trunk and, back and forth, they've
puzzled the suitcases in there, and now the driver laughs, and
they just get into their seats and in a moment are driving away.

Mira thinks she knows what she might write to Aisha,
whom she loves, even though the love, like anything she could
say, is of no use to anyone. She could write, Dear Aisha, do
you think love is a magical apple or cabbage you can keep
grating without destroying its roundness? And do you know
what happens to the dead when the living won't let them rest
in peace? Doesn't every story tell us this? The dead wander
the earth in pain and anger and grief, knocking over remote
controls and family portraits, rattling windowpanes in the
night. They suffer, and they make the living suffer. It's much
the same, I've learned, with love: once you've sent it to the
grave, whether in premeditated murder or sloppiness, you
shouldn't try to resurrect it, warm up the stiffened unwilling
limbs. It becomes a mess, in short. Like love, like the dead, you
and Bernard wander in pain and anger and grief — and, okay,
my analogies are unraveling, because I'm not a writer, only
an ordinary person struck by the complications of the whole
business. I don't want to pose as the wise elder either, because
I am neither wise nor, quite yet, old, and the last thing I want
to do is condescend to you, especially since I have learned of
what you had put up with from Bernard, which was all a bit of
surprise to me, and I feel I somehow must apologize for — but

anyway, I want to speak woman to woman, and woman: don't you think you have got to choose, because another thing that happens is that we die, this I'm sure you've felt in your bones too, we die, we die, we die, and look at us wasting our time?

It's got to end sometime, said Alice's dad, with some cheerfulness. Will that stead you? I miss the Adriatic, Dad said, meaning, I suppose, all the rest of it, too.

The mother with the red-headed girl pulls her purse over her shoulder and gets up, extends her hand for the girl to take. The girl ambles out of her seat, now with even some bounce in her step, and reaches for her mom. The spackled baguette is abandoned but the chocolate milk finished. The mom takes her by the wrist. The backs of the girl's knock-knees are white and fragile, beautiful and insistent as she walks away.

The dining room is empty now. Merima has already cleared most of the tables and carries a full tray of dishes to the back kitchen.

"Well," Bernard says, "last ones to leave."

Mira pours out the last of the coffee, splitting it between their two cups.

"Will you ask Merima about the pigeon?"

"Oh, I don't know. You should. She'll feel more sorry for you, with that eye."

In the hallway beyond the reception counter she glimpses the tall form of that one maid. What was her name?

Bernard follows her glance.

"Oh," he says.

"What was her name?"

"Mahue." The woman doesn't turn to look their way, disappears up the stairs, going about her business.

He shakes his head. "I wish you would talk to Merima about the pigeon. My Croatian will fail me, and I don't know if she speaks English."

"She'll accept it more easily from you. Me, she'll just think I'm weird, nursing a pigeon as it were a kitten or something."

"Let's both tell her."

"Okay. I'll talk, but I'll say the pigeon was your idea and you're embarrassed to ask."

"Fine."

When Merima is back in the dining room, Mira waves at her, in the most apologetic, friendliest way she can manage. Merima leaves her tray on the last dirty table and walks over.

"A pigeon? Just a pigeon from the street?"

"It's stupid, I know. We felt sorry for it."

Merima's smile is the smile you might direct at a child who just told you they built a secret hill out of whipped cream somewhere in the house — do you want to go find it? This is cute, the smile says, but how much of a headache did you just land in my life?

"It was my idea," says Bernard. "I convinced her."

Now Merima genuinely laughs.

"How much time have you got, when's your flight — you're checking out, right?"

"It's not until five something."

"If you give me a few minutes, I'll show you where I could put it."

They wait, both slowly sipping their coffees. When Merima returns, they follow her, cups in hand. They walk through the kitchen — was it just two nights ago I was in here desperately looking for juice, Bernard thinks? — to a low-ceilinged hall-way, damp-smelling. Merima pushes on a heavy door, and then they're in a courtyard. There are two small iron tables and chairs with plastic ashtrays on them, cracked concrete tile on the ground, a vine-covered wall, and an almost complete canopy of tree cover from lindens and chestnuts.

"Maybe here? It's pretty secluded. Staff come back here for breaks. We can check the bird's got water, etc."

"I like it," Bernard says. He turns toward Mira. "Right?"

"Gosh, yes, thank you."

"You can just bring it down, if you like. I've got to run back, but I'll take my coffee break here in a bit." Before she closes the door behind her, she adds, "Don't leave without saying goodbye, okay?"

When the door shuts, Bernard moves to see if it can be opened from the outside. It can, and he closes it again.

"Thank goodness," he says. He sits down in the nearest chair. "I'm so tired."

"We're lucky," Mira says.

Bernard reaches out toward the trunk of the large chest-nut near him. "Look at the size of this tree." He puts his hand on the bark.

Mira does too. She leans into it. She's reluctant to sit.

"Should we go up and get that box?"

"I'll go. Is that okay?"

She smiles at him. "I'll be here," she says.

He leaves and she stays leaning on the tree and is surprised to see the street beyond it, because she could see nothing but wall and foliage when they first stepped out. The view is narrow but the street wide and shimmering with sun. She looks down the long stretch of it. No trees, five stories of windows and white shutters and French doors on both sides. There are traces of yesterday's storm, small puddles at the edges of the road. There really was a storm. How lovely and quiet now. No one is in sight. She keeps listening for something but hears no footsteps and no voices. Clear. No, she won't see anyone she knows or knew on this street. The sky is an imprecise unravelling of cloud matter, white strings. But good lord, that sun gleaming on the puddles and the sidewalk and the bike posts. Shoots of weeds poking through the concrete, as they do, at the edge of the curb, here and there. It's starting again, the wild cleaving in her chest. Breathe. Bernard will be back in a moment, with his swollen eye, his cheek chafed. She is scared also. Yes yes. But. She grasps a thin branch at eye level, steps beyond the tree, into the opening leading to the street.

ACKNOWLEDGEMENTS

I'm very lucky this novel was embraced by Freehand Books. My sincere thanks go to the Freehand team, for their skill, professionalism, attention, good humour, and care. Thank you to Natalie Olsen for beautiful design and capturing the novel's aesthetic. Thank you to Colby Clair Stolson for thorough promotion work. Endless thank yous to Kelsey Attard, for graciously accommodating me again and again as I edited this novel on maternity leave and through sickness, and for lending her wisdom and generosity to every stage of the process.

Profound thanks to my editor, Deborah Willis, whose writing I've long admired. Her sharpness, depth of insight and understanding of the work, both in its spirit and in its details, improved the manuscript significantly and made me see it in new ways. Her kindness and generosity also made editing a pleasure.

I am indebted to my writing groups and friends. To Julie and Astrid and Tatiana, who read more versions and portions of this than anyone should, gave me smart comments, and made it possible for me to persevere — love and eternal thanks. Big thanks to Lisa, Will, Mat, Rebecca, Thea, and Becks, for reading and providing valuable advice and feedback. Love to dear Becks for all the many things. Love to Thea and Scott for their friendship and cheering me on. And love to my Lisa, whose talent for encouragement lifted me time and again, for sharing the whole journey. Warm thanks to Trisia for the photos. Much gratitude to my parents, for always being interested and supporting me in various ways. Kind thanks to Vinni, for generously sharing details of his family's journey from Vietnam to Canada. And much love to Greta and Adrian — for supporting, and inspiring, and for letting me borrow *bezombies,* among other things. Thank you also to all of Dan's lovely family.

Thank you to the Alberta Foundation for the Arts, for valuable and much appreciated financial support. Many thanks to Sage Hill and the people who run it, whose fiction program provided beautiful space and community. I'm especially grateful to Alissa York, Wonder Woman, who helped me make great progress on the manuscript, and whose spirit and words about writing continue to inspire me. And to the whole group at Sage Hill in 2016, who, it turned out, were not only awesome dancers and frisbee throwers, but smart readers too.

Love and thanks forever to Ben, for reading, and everything else — including letting me use his line, "first caffeine of the morning when our lives were surely past noon." I'm enormously grateful to Naomi Lewis, for her generous reading and feedback when I needed it most, and for championing the manuscript — love and more love to you.

Finally, all my love, now and always, to Dan, for being my everything, my ground and my cheer, for loving, reading, advising, and persisting through hard times. And to Dori and Flora, my hearts.

Two lines from Karen Solie's poem "Prayers for the Sick" appear in the manuscript, "Who've seen the early-season / potential of our childhood exhausted" on page 116, and "O Lord, you who cast low / and raise up also" on page 180, gratefully used with permission.

JASMINA ODOR is a Croatian-born Canadian writer, who emigrated to Canada in 1993. She is the author of the short story collection *You Can't Stay Here* (Thistledown Press, 2017), winner of the Canadian Authors Association Exporting Alberta Award. Her fiction and reviews have been widely published in magazines and anthologies, including *The New Quarterly, The Malahat Review, The Fiddlehead, Eighteen Bridges, Prism International*, and the *Journey Prize Stories*. Her short fiction has won the Howard O'Hagan Award and been nominated for the Journey Prize and the CBC Short Story Prize, among others. She lives with her family in Edmonton, on Treaty 6 territory, where she also teaches English literature and writing.